TIME OF DEATH
THE LAST SILK BLOT

josh anderson

E
EPIC
Press

The Last Silk Blot
Time of Death: Book #6

Written by Josh Anderson

Copyright © 2016 by Abdo Consulting Group, Inc.

Published by EPIC Press™
PO Box 398166
Minneapolis, MN 55439

Cover design by Dorothy Toth
Images for cover art obtained from iStockPhoto.com
Edited by Ramey Temple

LIBRARY OF CONGRESS CATALOGING-IN-PUBLICATION DATA

Anderson, Josh.
The last silk blot / Josh Anderson.
p. cm. — (Time of death ; #6)
Summary: When Kyle and Allaire travel outside the walls of the time tunnel, they
meet Kyle's ancient ancestor, and their journey takes a turn that he could have never
anticipated. Now, with everything on the line, Kyle must revisit the demons of the
past one final time if he was any hope of leaving them behind once and for all.
ISBN 978-1-68076-069-9 (hardcover)
1. Time travel—Fiction. 2. Traffic accidents—Fiction. 3. Life change events—Fiction. 4. Interpersonal relations—Fiction. 5. Conduct of life—Fiction.
6. Guilt—Fiction. 7. Self-acceptance—Fiction. 8. Young adult fiction. I. Title.
[Fic]—dc23
2015903989

To Mom,

Watching you achieve your dreams
inspired me to chase my own.

CHAPTER 1

about ten thousand years ago in serica

SIMYON USED HIS KNEE TO PUSH ONE OF THE larger hogs away from the runt. He'd learned that if he didn't hover over the smallest animal in the stone pig enclosure, she wouldn't get to eat at all and would likely die. He called the little pig "Delilah" and empathized with her place as the smallest member of her family.

"You know, Father will only kill her sooner if you make her fat," Umar said with a laugh. He sat across the pen, against the low stone wall, mindlessly tossing pebbles into the dirt in front of him.

Simyon shrugged. His older brother didn't understand. He never did. "Hey!" Simyon said, pushing away another big male hog with designs on Delilah's feed.

Once he was confident she'd gotten enough to eat, Simyon continued to the other feed baskets, filling them with scraps—mostly discarded garbage from their village. Simyon liked that hogs weren't picky like people.

When he heard a noise in the dirt behind him, Simyon turned and saw that Umar was tossing rocks in Delilah's direction. He didn't even look like he was getting any great joy from it, until Simyon took notice, of course.

"Stop it," Simyon said, blotting his head with the green handkerchief their father had given him.

Umar tossed another rock at the small pig.

Simyon's brother didn't even look his way. He'd picked up the tactic from his father, the head of their village, and a member of the Serican council. When he didn't like what one of the villagers said to him, his father proudly explained, the easiest solution was to avoid responding directly. "Talk only to the larger issues," their father would proclaim. "Never the trivialities." Simyon knew Delilah was a triviality to his brother.

He was about to tell Umar to stop again, but instead, Simyon picked up a rock at his feet and threw it toward Umar. Simyon had good enough aim to make sure he didn't hit his brother, but he made sure to land the rock close enough to make his point.

Now Umar took the stones and pebbles of various sizes he'd collected in his hand, reared back and threw them at Simyon, who turned his face away instinctively. Only a few small pebbles hit Simyon, the rest landing harmlessly in the dirt behind him. Umar never hesitated to be the aggressor, but he could turn his opinion of himself into that of the aggrieved party just as quickly.

Seconds after Simyon turned back to their joint duty of minding the hogs, Umar ran at him and tackled him from the side, sending the pigs scurrying away. Simyon had to be very careful about raising a hand to his older brother. Regardless of how justifiable, their father had put younger Serican men to death before for "lifting fists" to the heirs of their families. First-born sons were, in many ways, considered a cut above their siblings, and the rules were different for them.

Simyon tried to protect himself as they rolled on the ground. His brother was weak, but he had to let Umar get the upper hand and perhaps get a few punches in, before Simyon could even consider fighting back. Simyon rolled onto his back. As he did, though, he noticed that the wooden gate to the hog enclosure was open. "Wait!" Simyon screamed as his brother wound up to punch him in the face. Before he could speak, Umar delivered a punch to his left cheek, which rattled Simyon's head. Their father would actually be proud of Umar for disciplining his two-years-younger brother. The matter at hand leading to their fight would never be discussed.

After the momentary shock of the punch to the

face faded, Simyon yelled to his brother again and pointed at the gate. "Wait! Look!"

Umar stood up slowly—like he did everything—and the young men watched as Delilah and the largest male hog ran to the grass outside.

Simyon ran out of the enclosure after them, waited for his brother behind him, and then shut and latched the gate. They each grabbed a swine herder's stick as they watched the hogs race across the field in the direction of Serican Point.

"Run!" Simyon called out, pulling his brother by the shirt. "Father will whip us if we—"

"You're such a fool," Umar answered, again following after his younger brother.

They ran after the hogs, but the spooked animals sped further ahead every second. Simyon felt regret as he ran. Knowing the animals could be spooked so easily, he never should've let the matter with Umar escalate in the enclosure. *Why did I throw that rock?* he thought to himself. He'd let much larger indignities go before. There was something about watching his brother take aim at defenseless Delilah, who had to take it from her own kind as well, that reminded Simyon of how much he wished his brother was not his brother.

They barely kept the hogs in sight as they chased behind them. The animals were still headed straight toward Serican Point, the sound of the sacred river below getting louder as the brothers got closer.

Simyon and Umar were going to have no choice but to try to corner the hogs at one of the cliff edges. But, when they reached the natural stone arch leading into Serican Point, Umar stopped running.

"Let's wait for them here," Umar said.

"Wait? It could be days," Simyon said. "What will we tell Father? He'll come to get the large one for slaughter soon. Perhaps this afternoon." The consequence for losing the hogs would be much worse than leaving the family's property without their father's permission.

"You care more about the small one," Umar

said, "because you're weak. Even our sister thinks so."

Simyon passed through the natural doorway to Serican Point. "Fine. You stay here. I'll chase them in this direction. Can you handle both of them?"

"Of course I can herd two swine, you idiot," Umar said, holding his swine herder's stick in front of him as if he thought Simyon had forgotten he had it.

Simyon walked in the direction of the hogs on the thinning landscape in front of him. To his left and right were sheer cliffs. Beneath the right side of the cliff were the jagged, chalky rocks commonly seen throughout the Serican landscape. The area was completely inaccessible by humans, but now and then someone gazing down at the rocks might catch sight of wild mountain goats. On the left, there was an equally long drop that led to the sacred river rushing below. Even though their father's property practically overlooked it, neither of them had ever swam or bathed in it. One of the first rules their father ever gave the boys was that no person was ever allowed to touch the water of sacred river. Their father was not one to explain his rules, but the boys knew that they weren't the only ones bound by this rule. Throughout Serica, entering the sacred river was known to be among the worst transgressions a person could commit.

The large hog was sniffing the grass right at the edge of the right side of the cliff. Simyon was afraid of spooking the animal too much and sending it running off the cliff to its death on the rocks below. It wasn't impossible that a hog could accidentally walk off a cliff, which would enrage their father, who would trade portions of the pig to other villagers in exchange for other food and family necessities. Simyon also had no confidence in Umar taking any responsibility at all if they lost one of the animals.

Just as Simyon wondered whether the large hog might actually walk over the cliff, he saw Delilah, even more dangerously close to the edge, but on the left side, over the water. He looked toward the larger hog and knew that it should be the priority. It was nearly ready for slaughter and if they could only save one, their father would be less furious if they lost Delilah than the larger hog.

But Simyon walked slowly toward the smaller pig, hoping to loop further toward the pointed edge of the cliff before she took notice of him. He could then hook around her with his stick and try to guide her toward the stone arch.

Just as he tried passing quietly by Delilah, he heard footsteps behind him and turned to see Umar with a panicked look on his face. If his brother could mess something up for him, it inevitably would come to pass.

"It's Father" Umar said. "He's heading toward the pig pen."

Simyon tried to think. Their father would probably be able to easily coax both hogs back to the enclosure, but the beatings for the boys, especially Simyon, if Umar could find a way to pin this completely on him, would be severe. Still, though, it would be better than losing the pigs. "Call for him!"

"Are you crazy?" Umar asked, smirking at Simyon. "No. Father will respect us only if we clean up our own mess."

Umar ran toward the larger hog, swineherd's stick in his hand. The large male looked up when he heard Umar's footsteps and the pig shuffled to the side. Simyon cringed when Umar stumbled, causing the hog to rear up on its back legs. As it did, its back legs dug into the unstable grass right at the cliff face and Simyon watched the dirt fall backward down to the rocks below. An instant later, the hog's back legs slipped from the cliff, and in a flash, the large male was gone. Simyon ran toward his brother, and the two of them crept carefully toward the edge.

The large hog was on its side, dead, nearly fifty feet down. "I can climb," Simyon said, but he knew he could not.

"You're such a fool," Umar said. "We need to go."

"Where?" Simyon asked.

"Anywhere," Umar answered. "If we deny being responsible, Father may suspect. But he won't punish us."

Umar was right. Their father could be brutal in meting out punishment, not only to the villagers over whom he presided, but to his family as well. But, given his official position, he had rules to follow, and he never punished anyone without clear evidence of wrongdoing.

Umar ran to the other side of Serican Point and looked down to the river. When he ran over, Delilah started back toward the stone arch, heading in the direction of the pig enclosure. "If father sees her running back from this direction, he'll come here looking for us."

Simyon was glad to see Delilah heading back. He wracked his brain for what they could do to avoid punishment. Being whipped was so excruciating that it inspired all manner of creativity to avoid it.

"The river is deep," Umar said. "We would survive the jump."

Simyon looked down at the sacred river. He'd never considered its depth, only the impossibility of ever going in it. "How do you know the river is deep?"

Umar looked at him and wrinkled his brow. "I don't know. I just do."

"You've been in the sacred river?" Simyon asked.

"Don't be so quick to believe Father's stories," Umar said.

Simyon watched as Delilah went all the way through the stone arch. Their father would come this way soon. "It's not just Father. No one goes into the sacred river, Umar." Simyon wasn't so sure he believed that his brother had gone in before. While Umar wasn't exactly diligent about following the rules, he also wasn't brave.

Simyon looked down at the strong current of

the river rushing away from their village. To escape from their father's detection now, jumping might be their only option. Simyon looked toward the stone arch, and then down again. He shook his head. "We should just admit what happened."

Umar smiled at him. "You'll go back by yourself then. Later, I'll tell him I had nothing to do with this. I'll tell him this happened because you were trying to make love to the little pig."

"He won't believe you," Simyon said, disgusted by his brother, but not surprised.

"It won't matter, second son," Umar answered, still smirking. "You'll be there admitting guilt, and I'll come back in an hour and deny everything . . . It's time for a bath anyway."

Simyon looked at his brother, but could barely summon rage anymore. He was so used to being angry with Umar, it was just the prevailing emotion he carried into their interactions.

"Don't be such a fool," Umar said. Then he stepped back a few steps, looked at his brother once more, and ran off the edge of the cliff toward the water below.

Simyon watched his brother's body plummet through the air. A few seconds later, Umar popped up in the river waving his arms, the current in the water already pulling him east. Simyon couldn't believe his brother was in the sacred river. They'd pretended as children to throw their enemies down there to watch their skin burn off. But, there was Umar, safe as he could be, given the strong current in the river.

Simyon looked again toward the stone arch. He touched the spot on the back of his leg that still hurt from one of father's whippings months ago. He took a few steps back. He knew the longer he thought about it, the more likely it was that he'd just talk himself out of jumping. He closed his eyes and ran full speed until there was no more of Serican Point beneath his feet. The fall felt endless as he clenched and waited to hit the cold water. As soon as he did, he felt sure he'd made a mistake. Following Umar was never the best choice.

Once Simyon popped back up to the surface of the river, he spotted Umar, holding onto a boulder poking out from the river's surface. Simyon grabbed onto it as well. The river didn't feel any different to him than the Coquish River where they normally bathed, except for the pull being a bit stronger.

"I'm surprised," Umar said, panting a bit. "You're usually so weak."

Simyon ignored the insult and held tightly to the boulder. His let his legs give in to the pull of the river while he clung to his spot with his arms.

Umar pointed at a spot on the riverbank. "Let's go."

"Hold on," Simyon answered. "Let's rest a minute. Look at the pull over there. What if we go to the other side? We can take the bridge down the way over the river."

"Weakling," Umar said, shaking his head. "That

would take twice as much time." He jumped out into the river.

Simyon wanted to stay close in the strong current, and he followed his brother.

As soon as he started swimming, he knew they were never going to hit their target. Simyon saw Umar's head go under the water, and then pop up. He was spinning in some sort of circular current, turning again and again. He saw the look of panic on his face and Simyon swam toward him, hoping he could pull him out of it.

But when Simyon reached Umar, he started spinning too. It was like a twisting wind, but inside the water. After about a minute of fruitlessly trying to swim out of this strange circular current, Simyon felt the water pulling him underneath. He took as big a breath as he could and had no choice but to submit. *Father was right all along*, Simyon thought to himself.

He felt sad that his mother would never know what happened to him if he drowned here and his body never washed up. The Seres were not a culture that mourned or remarked much about death. Mostly, they just waited for it expectantly. It was irrelevant to the dead, but sometimes hard on the close relations of the deceased, who were expected to move on from their grief quickly.

Once he was pulled underneath the water, his arms and legs fighting against the pull, Simyon felt like he was freefalling, moving much too quickly to be in the water, he thought. He screamed and surprisingly, could hear himself clearly. He even opened his eyes, and instead of feeling the burn of river water, he saw only a silver blur passing by. He had the same feeling he had when jumping from the cliff, except this time it felt endless. After feeling like he was freefalling for several minutes, Simyon wondered if he were dead and would experience this falling sensation for the rest of eternity.

When Simyon woke up later, on his back in the sand, inside a deep trench in the ground, he had no idea how long he'd been unconscious. He looked next to him and Umar was laying there as well, also beginning to sit up, as if awakening from a long and deep sleep. It was bright out, but he couldn't see the sun, and noticed that the sky had a purple wash over it, like an extreme sunset.

"What happened?" Umar asked, the normal assuredness in his voice gone.

Simyon stood up, but had no words to offer his brother. He looked up over the edge of the trench they were in and saw the water on one side and more sand on the other side, leading to a grassy hill. This looked nothing like anywhere he knew of in Serica.

"You're not in Serica," a voice above them said, as if it had been listening to Simyon's thoughts.

Both boys looked up and saw an old man dressed in unusual clothing bending over the edge of the trench, his hands on his knees. He wore a shirt with buttons and flowing pants, as opposed to the traditional double-layer Serican robe and stocking combination.

"You're not supposed to be here," the Old Man said, grimacing as he shook his head. "Your being here is a very bad thing."

Simyon looked to Umar, the older brother expected to speak for their family when meeting unfamiliar strangers. But Umar just stared at the man, and then past him to the purple sky. *A purple sky?* Their father's travels had brought them through nearly all of Serica, but rarely past its borders.

"Where are we?" Simyon asked.

The Old Man didn't say anything but reached out his hand. Simyon grabbed it first and the Old Man helped him climb out of the trench. Then, he did the same for Umar.

The Old Man stopped and sized the young men up as they stood beside each other. The Old Man nodded to himself as if he'd made a decision.

"Our father will be looking for us," Umar said to him.

The Old Man's face didn't move. "And he will find you, Umar. Now, I don't imagine you have much to say to each other?

"Us?" Umar asked, pointing to Simyon.

"Yes," the Old Man answered, "seeing as this is goodbye?"

Simyon looked at Umar, whose confused look matched his. Brothers united, for once.

"I'm going to lead Umar back to your father," the Old Man said. "After I do, you'll never see each other again."

"I don't understand," Simyon said. "Wait! What's happening here?"

The Old Man looked at each of them and shook his head. It almost looked to Simyon like he might reconsider.

"You went into the sacred river. You were never supposed to come here," The Old Man said.

"I'm sorry," Simyon said. "I'm sorry. We'll never do it again."

Umar just looked at the Old Man with wide eyes, too stunned to talk.

"We can't just have people trespassing here," the Old Man said. "My hands are tied."

Simyon shook his head. "Where are you taking him?"

"He's going back home," the Old Man said.

"What about me?" Simyon asked, frantically trying to understand what was happening.

"You're staying here," the Old Man answered.

"Why?" Simyon asked. "Why do I have to stay here?"

The Old Man cracked a slight smile. "Because I don't want *him*. Now, is there anything either of you want to impart to the other? This is your last opportunity."

Umar shrugged. Simyon couldn't believe Umar was just going to stand there and let this happen.

"What will you tell Father?" Simyon asked.

Just then, the Old Man stepped forward and put his forefinger on the space right under Umar's nose, right above his mouth. Simyon could see smoke coming from the area the Old Man was touching.

Umar moaned at first from the pain. But, it rose quickly to a scream louder than anything Simyon had ever heard. All the while, the Old Man just kept his finger in place.

When the Old Man removed his finger, he grabbed Umar by the neck of his robe and threw him into the trench, jumping in after him. He picked Umar up, again by his robe, and the two of them walked through the trench together. Umar looked up at Simyon once more, the brothers sharing a look not quite of warmth, more of just familiarity. Simyon noticed that Umar now had a strange indentation in the space above his mouth.

Simyon stood watching and bent over the trench as Umar and the Old Man moved into the distance. He wondered for a moment where he was, and what had happened. But, as he watched the Old Man and Umar walk further and further into the trench, Simyon realized he knew exactly where he was. He knew what he was supposed to, but not why. He could suddenly see many generations into the future, his descendants on this very beach, building a strong metal tunnel. Would the Old Man tell him why he was there? Why his people, forevermore, would be involuntarily drafted to work here?

He felt hot breath on his neck, which made him jump. When he turned, he saw a woman. She was beautiful and he could feel strength radiating from her. It was almost uncomfortable to be so close, even as he immediately ached to touch her body, which was draped only in a fine silk. He knew the quality of the silk was as good as anything the Sericans could produce. Her orange hair shot curls in every direction, and her green eyes looked straight into Simyon's. He could see the curves of her body perfectly under the thin silk. He hadn't known that any civilization on earth could produce a blue silk of this quality.

"You are not a Sere anymore," she said. "We'll start a new tradition together."

The woman took his hand and led him away from the trench.

Simyon looked back and didn't see Umar or the Old Man anymore. He looked again now at the woman's body, and again, he knew exactly what he was supposed to do. Not *why*, but that didn't matter much at all to him in that moment.

CHAPTER 2

OUTSIDE OF TIME

moments after kyle broke through the tunnel

A FEW MINUTES AFTER HE AND THE MAN ON THE other side started chipping away at the tunnel with their paddles, Kyle stepped through the hole they had made. He stood in a trench outside the tunnel now, and looked up at a purple, sunless sky.

The man with the green, silk handkerchief wrapped around his head tossed his paddle up to the ground above and climbed easily out of the trench, where he joined a group of about twenty other people. Kyle started to follow, but his foot slipped when he tried to climb the steep trench.

"Hold on," the man said, bracing himself into a crouch, and then holding his hand out for Kyle.

Kyle grabbed onto the man's hand, grunted, and pulled himself up onto the sandy beach. "Thanks."

"If you don't know the footholds, it's too steep to climb out on your own," the man said dryly. "Who are you?"

Kyle looked around. The people behind the man also wore shabby clothes, and eyed Kyle conspicuously. "I'm Kyle Cash. Where is this? When is this?"

"I'm Simyon," the man said, stepping forward. His expression was wary and serious. "My brother was Umar. Do you know who he is? Or, who he was?"

"Who?" Kyle asked.

"Umar . . . My brother," Simyon said. "It's been a long time since I've seen him."

Kyle shook his head. "I'm sorry, no. Can someone please tell me where I am? Who's in charge here? Maybe I should speak to them?"

"These are my people," Simyon said. "And

you're the first person from the other side who's come here in a very long time."

"What's 'the other side'?" Kyle asked. He looked at Simyon and the people behind him and noticed there was something different about them, but he couldn't place it. Something was different about the way they looked.

"Your world," Simyon answered. "Where you came from."

Kyle turned around now and saw the tunnel from the outside for the first time. He was surprised at how black the exterior was. Most of it was covered with branches and leaves, but where the metal peeked out, Kyle could see that it shimmered in the same way as a silk blot. Thousands of people were working near the tunnel, with primitive looking equipment—pulleys, hoisting machines, shovels, and rakes. Some pulled branches off of the tunnel. Others worked together to carry huge, curved sections of tunnel away from the worksite. The part he had broken through was a wall at the end of the tunnel. "Why is the tunnel shrinking?" Kyle asked. "Are they taking it apart? They have to stop. Right now."

Simyon smiled at him, then reached his finger gently to Kyle's face and ran his finger along the space between Kyle's top lip and his nose. He gently pressed against Kyle's philtrum—the little indentation under his nose. "You've got one too . . ." Kyle noticed then that the area under Simyon's nose was completely flat with no philtrum at all.

"Please," Kyle said. "They need to stop, or I think my world is going to end. Why would you want to hurt people?"

Simyon shook his head. "I don't want to hurt anyone . . . Most of my people would do anything if it meant they could cross over to the other side. But, we're paying a debt here. We can't just *stop*."

"What debt?" Kyle asked. "Why do you have to take the tunnel apart?"

Simyon took a deep breath and looked off for a moment, as if he was considering how much to share with Kyle. "A long time ago . . . A *very* long time ago, my brother and I found this place. We were chasing a pig. We were never supposed to be here. No human was. As punishment for trespassing, I had to stay here and build the tunnel."

"And what about all of these people?" Kyle asked, pointing behind Simyon and then down the beach at all of the workers. "Did they trespass too?"

Simyon shook his head. "They're all my descendants. They've been forced to pay for my mistake as well. And they hate me for it."

Kyle looked at all of Simyon's people, working on the tunnel like an experienced construction crew. There were at least a thousand of them, all constantly moving, except for one older man, sitting away from the others, reclining up on a small, grassy hillside. "How long have you—?"

"We've been building the tunnel for many generations," Simyon said. "I don't like taking it apart any more than you do."

Kyle looked at Simyon and considered what he

was saying. He barely seemed older than Kyle. At most, he looked about twenty. "For generations? These are your *descendants?*"

"If you're here," Simyon said, "then you understand that time is more flexible than people on the other side think it is."

"You have to stop taking the tunnel apart," Kyle said. "Please."

"I don't know what to tell you," Simyon said.

"Who's he?" Kyle asked, pointing at the old man on the hillside.

"No one," Simyon answered.

Kyle could tell from Simyon's face that he was lying. "Bullshit." He pushed past Simyon and started in the direction of the man on the hill, but two of the other people—a man with thick arms, and a woman with dark hair and sad eyes— grabbed Kyle by the arms. "Let me go!"

"You should go back to the other side while you still can," Simyon said.

Kyle didn't realize until he saw it in the dark-haired woman's hand that she'd taken the wooden paddle from his pocket. He tried grabbing it back, but the man pushed him in the chest away from her, sending Kyle stumbling back to the ground. He noticed the sand underneath his hands felt different than any beach he'd ever been on. It felt lighter and less substantial.

Looking up at the people standing over him, again, Kyle tried to put his finger on what it was that felt slightly off about them. Then, he realized it. Just like Simyon, they were missing their philtrums. All of Simyon's people were without them. Kyle reached up and felt his own and saw Simyon take notice. He wondered why these otherwise normal looking people all shared this one peculiarity.

"There's no need for violence here," Simyon said, walking over and offering Kyle his hand again. "I'm sure it's frustrating to not get the answers you're seeking."

Kyle nodded. He felt pessimistic now about whether he was going to get any answers at all.

He didn't believe for a second that Simyon was really in charge, even though his people seemed to support him. He pointed out to a thick line of trees, up from the beach. "What's up there?"

Simyon shook his head. "You can't go there. No one can."

Kyle looked down the beach at the tunnel, which stretched all the way to the horizon. "Where *can* I go? I need some answers."

Simyon shrugged. "You're welcome to sit on the beach for a little while. I can get you a meal, but then you'll need to go."

"I don't think you understand," Kyle said. "I'm not leaving until someone tells me why the tunnel is shrinking."

"You can see that it's *not* shrinking," Simyon said. "My people are taking it apart."

"Are you a Sere?" Kyle asked.

Simyon shook his head. "I was. Now, I'm not sure what I am."

Kyle was beyond confused and quickly tiring

of the runaround Simyon was giving him. He wanted to demand straight answers. But, he was outnumbered too, and wasn't going to be able to go anywhere the group didn't want him to.

"I'll wait here for answers," Kyle said. "Tell whoever's in charge that I'll be right here—"

"I told you, I'm in charge," Simyon said. "I have responsibilities here, and I can't—"

"If you were in charge," Kyle said, "you'd have better answers."

"Don't be so sure," Simyon answered.

"Tell whoever it is you answer to—whoever told you to take the tunnel apart—that I have responsibilities too. And I'm not leaving until someone tells me why your people are doing something that will cause catastrophe in my world." Kyle sat down defiantly in the sand, and pulled his knees to his chest.

Simyon stood over him for a moment and then nodded. Without a word, he turned around, and the people behind him followed. The dark-haired woman with sad eyes bent down to Kyle. She was beautiful—unblemished, like she was created in a computer program. "What's it like on the other side?"

Kyle thought about how to answer. "I don't—"

"Rosalee," one of the other women snapped. "Let's go!"

The woman nodded at Kyle, tossed his paddle into the sand next to him, and walked away, leaving him by himself, staring out at the water, and the empty trench in front of it, where a section of the tunnel used to sit.

CHAPTER 3

OUTSIDE OF TIME

later that day

KYLE SAT IN THE SAND FOR HOURS, WATCHING the workers methodically disassemble the tunnel until their workday ended and the sky turned from a vague purple to a deep violet. Almost in unison, all of Simyon's people stopped what they were doing and walked down the beach together with the slow amble Kyle imagined was the result of sheer exhaustion.

Kyle knew that questions like *where* or *when* were pointless here. For all of the unlikely things he'd seen since he first began time weaving, he'd never left the world he knew. But, there was no question that he was now somewhere outside the boundaries of the world he understood. Even in 2060, the imperiled world more or less resembled something Kyle knew. Kyle was exhausted and knew he likely wouldn't get any more answers until the people awoke and work began again on dismantling the tunnel. But, Kyle's mind was far too active to sleep. He had a sense that he was nearing the end of his incredible journey, and sleep was the furthest thing from his mind.

He stood up and looked at the huge worksite along the beach. Beyond that, he could see what looked like a vast, dark ocean, except there were no waves. It was the quietest beach Kyle had ever heard. He stood up and walked toward the water to get a closer look.

When he reached the huge trench, Kyle turned onto his stomach and climbed down. Inside the trench, he saw scattered mulberry leaves and branches, and silkworms clinging to their only food source. For whatever was different about this world, silkworms still depended on mulberry leaves. Kyle stepped carefully around the worms he could see, and began climbing up the other side of the trench. He dug his hands into the gristly sand and pulled up. It took a while to find the proper footing, but eventually, Kyle was able to make his way out to the narrow stretch of sand between the trench and the water.

Kyle noticed that, along with the absence of waves, the sand wasn't any wetter near the water. Even just a foot from the waterline, the sand was as soft and dry. He bent down to the water and stuck his hand in. It was a little colder than he might've expected, but what struck Kyle was that it felt thicker. It was more like sticking his hand in pancake batter. When he pulled his hand out, though, the thick liquid dripped right off like water.

He looked up at the starless sky, which, even in darkness, had a violet tint to it. There was a lack of depth he'd never noticed on "his side." The night sky always felt infinite to Kyle at home, even on a cloudy night when the moon was the only hard evidence of the enormity of the galaxy.

After a while, Kyle stood up again and headed back over the trench. He walked along a segment of the tunnel that hadn't yet been dismantled and came to a camp. There were fifty or sixty low, rectangular tents of varying sizes. All of them were the same tan color, and some had the faint glow of candlelight inside. All the scene needed was a campfire surrounded by happy vacationers and it would've looked like an advertisement in an outdoor catalog.

All of the tents were completely shut, except one. Kyle could see a sliver of activity inside and found himself unable to avert his eyes. For all of the wonder of this different dimension, or wherever Kyle was, seeing a simple, everyday interaction between two people was the most fascinating thing of all. *Their life is here*, Kyle thought to himself. *This is their world.*

He saw a man and woman inside the tent speaking

to each other with a child sleeping between them. The man looked like he was trying to explain something, and the woman had a slightly defensive posture. Kyle thought about Allaire, pregnant with their child, and hoped he'd be able to preserve their world and get back to her. When the woman in the tent suddenly turned and saw Kyle staring inside, she quickly crawled over to the tent's opening and shut it. Kyle felt embarrassed for intruding, but his curiosity was so great he couldn't help himself.

Kyle turned and walked up to the grassy area above the beach. He spotted another camp further down the beach as well, which looked as quiet as the one he'd just passed through. Kyle walked toward the thick tree line beyond the grass and stopped for a second. He listened for the outdoor noises he was accustomed to hearing in the evenings, but again, the typical sounds were nowhere to be heard. There were no crickets chirping, no rodents rustling. While the place *looked* mostly like somewhere that might exist in Kyle's world, the lack of ambient noise was striking to him—one of those things he never would've thought about until it was gone.

He was about to enter the eerie silence of the tree line when he heard a voice coming from behind him.

"Don't!" the voice called out.

He turned and saw Rosalee standing there. She was the woman with the sad eyes who had spoken to him earlier.

"No one's ever come back from the trees," she said.

"What *is* this place?" Kyle asked, walking closer to her.

"This place is very uninteresting," Rosalee said. "Everything you see is exactly what it is. There's nothing more. At least, nothing we're allowed to see. I bet your world's much more interesting. It has to be. Please tell me what it's like . . . "

Kyle tried to think of how to describe the entirety of life on Earth and struggled to come up with anything. If this world was really as limited as what Kyle could see, then there was very little about his world he could explain that Rosalee would even understand. "I don't know . . . The sky isn't purple, and the ocean is rougher."

"Rougher?" Rosalee answered. Her face was much more relaxed now than when Kyle saw her before.

"We have waves in the ocean," Kyle said, pointing at the water. "It's never just still like this. It's constantly moving."

Rosalee cracked a smile. "What else?"

"I don't know," Kyle said. "Um . . . Everyone walks around with their head down looking at their phones. That's different than here."

"I don't know what—" Rosalee started, but then her eyes darted to her left and her entire expression changed.

Simyon was there now, standing only a few feet away from her. He must've crept up the hill without either of them noticing.

"You can't go in there," he said to Kyle. "The trees are not part of our territory."

Kyle glared at Simyon and shook his head. "You said you couldn't help me, but you're also telling me I can't go looking for answers on my own."

"Just go back to the beach," Simyon said. "We'll talk more in the morning."

Kyle wondered if turning his back on Simyon and heading into the trees would be a faster path to getting the answers he needed, but he considered that this wasn't his world. He didn't know the laws. Regardless of what seemed unreasonable to Kyle, for all he knew, Simyon might kill him if he defied him here.

As Kyle walked away back toward the beach, he turned around and saw Simyon angrily holding Rosalee by the shoulders as he spoke to her. Kyle stopped and looked at them, wondering for a moment if he'd need to intervene.

When Simyon saw him watching, he let go of Rosalee and they walked separately back toward the beach. The relaxed look Kyle had briefly spotted on Rosalee's face was gone.

Kyle was so tired that he eventually passed out on the beach waiting for morning to come. He awoke when the sky was a faded lavender color again, and Simyon's people were already back to work on the tunnel. Kyle shook his head as he watched the work progressing. The tunnel was still huge, extending well past where Kyle could see on the endless beach. But, if he couldn't find a way to stop them, 2017—the year he'd entered the tunnel—might not even be there when Kyle was ready to return. He wondered where all of the different timestreams went. And where had the years that had already been removed from the tunnel gone? Kyle wondered if the experiences of the billions of people who'd lived in these times had just evaporated into thin air.

He heard a shuffling in the sand and saw Rosalee

again, walking toward him holding something in her hands. She sat down in the sand and handed Kyle a bowl. It was filled with cut pieces of a blue fruit he'd never seen before.

Kyle eyed the fruit cautiously.

"It tastes like whatever you want it to," Rosalee said. She still had a nervous expression on her face, and Kyle realized that it must be her natural expression.

Kyle picked up a piece of fruit with his finger. "What do you mean?"

"What's your favorite food?" she asked.

"Uh . . . Pizza, I guess," Kyle answered.

"Okay," she said. "Try it."

Kyle took a bite of the fruit, which had the texture of a melon. Sure enough it tasted like pizza, but the texture made it strange. "I don't know if pizza was meant to be a fruit."

"I've never had pizza," she said. "We only have fruit here, so we just imagine the blue melon tastes like the fruit we like best."

"Okay, watermelon," Kyle said, taking another bite. It tasted just like watermelon, even if the consistency of the melon was closer to cantaloupe.

Rosalee giggled, and the tension of her face let up again. "You don't have to say what you want it to taste like. The fruit will work with your subconscious to taste like whatever will be most pleasing."

"Cool trick," Kyle said. "I'm sorry about last night. I wish I hadn't gotten you in trouble."

Rosalee surprised Kyle by laughing. "If I worried about disappointing Simyon, I'd *really* be in trouble . . . He needs to do things from time to time to show himself he's in charge. That's all."

Kyle considered this, and it fit with what he saw of Simyon: a leader, but an insecure one on shaky ground with his people.

Rosalee leaned her head closer to Kyle. "Do you think you'll consider staying?"

Kyle was taken aback. He hadn't even considered the possibility. "No. I have people back on—"

"The other side," Rosalee said.

Kyle noticed Rosalee's already sad face get a little sadder. He realized that telling her he had things to go back to in his world was like explaining that he had dinner plans to someone who had never even eaten before. "I'm sorry."

"It's okay," she said. "I'm happy you have a good life there."

"Can you help me?" Kyle asked.

Rosalee shrugged. "I don't know anything . . . Building this tunnel has taken my entire life. Nine generations now. Then we got the order to pull it apart. No one is happy, but we don't dare disobey."

"Why not? Who's in charge?" Kyle asked.

"I'm surprised it's you, Kyle, and not Demetrius who found a way to bridge our worlds," Rosalee said, picking up the paddle from the sand between them.

Kyle looked at the ancient Serican writing on the paddle as she traced the letters with her finger. "Did you know Demetrius? Did he come here too?

Someone I'm . . . Someone I'm very close to on the other side knew him well before he died."

"Died?" she said. "When?"

"A long time ago," Kyle answered.

"Oh," she said, nodding as she looked at the paddle. "There are two Demetriuses on here."

"See," she said, pointing to a row of letters fourth from the bottom. Then, she slid her finger to the last row on the paddle. "And here."

"Those are names?" Kyle asked.

Rosalee nodded. "Here's yours." She pointed to the next-to-last line.

"And the next one is 'Demetrius'?" Kyle asked.

Rosalee nodded.

"What do the names mean?" he asked.

"The people listed on here are Sere caretakers," Rosalee said. "On your side, people can perish, so there needs to be a list. Simyon's paddle has only his name because no one dies here."

Kyle took the paddle in his hand and looked at

the mysterious characters, shocked to know that even his own name was on there.

"So, Simyon really is in charge?" he asked.

"I've said too much already," she said.

Kyle looked at her, pleading with his eyes. "Please . . . It sounds like you'd like to cross over one day—"

"That'll never happen, Kyle," Rosalee said.

"I've seen a lot of things I thought would never happen," Kyle said. "Please . . . There won't be an 'other side' if I can't get your people to stop pulling the tunnel apart."

Rosalee stood up. "Please, don't tell them I said anything. Okay?"

Kyle looked down at the sand, disappointed. Even someone who tried to help him didn't have any answers that brought him closer to understanding why they were pulling the tunnel apart.

"Okay?" she asked again.

Kyle nodded. "Thanks for—"

"Good," she said, crouching down. "Keep my

name out of it . . . You need to talk to the Old Man on the hill. He barely even speaks to Simyon, and Simyon sometimes tries to pretend he's not getting his orders from him, but he is. The man on the hill is the key. He has all of the answers you want."

Rosalee stood up and quickly walked away from Kyle.

CHAPTER 4

OUTSIDE OF TIME

a few minutes later

KYLE WAITED A WHILE UNTIL HE SAW SIMYON occupied with a crew of workers pulling roots from the trench underneath a segment of the tunnel. Just like yesterday, the Old Man sat on the side of the hill. He lay back on his elbows, taking in the activity of the people below like someone in the midst of a long, lazy day.

Kyle stood up and began walking toward the hillside, making an effort to move at a fast clip, knowing that Simyon might try to stop him if he noticed.

Sure enough, as Kyle got within about thirty yards of the Old Man, Simyon caught up with him and put his hand on Kyle's shoulder.

"Get off of me," Kyle said.

"Please," Simyon said.

Kyle kept walking, as Simyon's grip got stronger.

"Don't do this, please," Simyon said, stepping in front of Kyle.

"You had a chance to give me answers," Kyle said. "You didn't."

Simyon leaned toward him and spoke quietly through gritted teeth. "Please make it look like we're having a friendly discussion."

"Why?" Kyle asked. "So it's easier to keep me away from him? He's in charge here, not you."

"Just calm down," Simyon said. "I sent you food. I let you stay on the beach. Please accept those as the good will gestures they were."

"I need to see him," Kyle said.

Simyon's shoulders slumped forward a little, his posture deflated. "Okay. I'll talk to him."

"No, *I'll* talk to him," Kyle said, trying to push past.

Simyon put a firm hand on Kyle's chest. "Don't.

I will talk to him and see how he wants to handle this, alright?"

Kyle took a deep breath and reluctantly shrugged. The Old Man was sitting right there watching them. Kyle couldn't understand why he wasn't able to speak with him. But Kyle hadn't come this far to leave without a way to stop the tunnel from shrinking, and if this was the only way he was going to make progress, he didn't have a choice.

"Now, just hold on. And stay here for a minute, please," Simyon said, before he turned and walked slowly up the hillside toward the Old Man. Kyle noticed how tentatively Simyon approached him. At first Simyon stood over him awkwardly, not sitting until the Old Man gestured for it.

Kyle watched them speak. He saw the Old Man shift his eyes in Kyle's direction, but he made no acknowledgment of him. It looked like Simyon was doing all of the speaking. From time to time, the Old Man would look over to him, but Kyle couldn't tell what his expression meant. Simyon spoke for another minute or two, and then Kyle saw the Old Man say something which caused Simyon to spring up quickly and move down the hill in a hurry toward Kyle.

"I'm sorry," Simyon said.

"What did he say?" Kyle asked.

Simyon put his hand on Kyle's shoulder and tried turning him away from the hillside toward the beach. "Come this way."

Kyle brushed his hand away. "I'm not going anywhere . . . What did he say?"

"He's not going to see you," Simyon said. "His decision is final."

"Does he know I came from the other side?" Kyle asked, using the parlance he'd heard Rosalee use.

"Of course he does," Simyon said, using his head to gesture down toward the beach. "He wants you to go back, which is exactly what I knew he would say . . . I can't emphasize enough how much you don't want to anger him."

Kyle smiled, unafraid now of breaching decorum with Simyon. "Listen, I don't know who you think you are, or who he is, but I can't emphasize how much I don't give a shit who I anger right now. I've got one job, and it's a damn important one. So, I'm not taking 'no' for an answer."

"I've tried being polite," Simyon said. "He won't like this, but I'm going to have to make you head back to the other side now. Let's go." Simyon put his hand on Kyle's lower back and pushed more firmly now.

Kyle smiled. "You still don't get it." He reared back and swung a haymaker at Simyon, knocking him into the sand. But when Kyle turned back, the Old Man was no longer on the hillside.

Kyle spotted the tree line and thought back to the night before when Simyon told him he needed to stay away. He started toward the thick foliage. All he could see on the other side of it was more purple sky peeking through the leaves.

"No, Kyle," Simyon called after him from the

ground. "Please don't. He'll . . . I don't know what he'll do . . . He watches everything. There is so much to watch. To him, beginnings and ends and life and death, they're trivial. Very small."

Kyle looked back at Simyon once more and then turned toward the trees.

"You've been passing up some good advice, Kyle," the Old Man said, suddenly appearing directly in front of Kyle. "You're not supposed to be here."

"I haven't even told you why I'm here," Kyle said.

The Old Man wrinkled his brow. "Give me a little more credit than that, Kyle."

"Where are we?" Kyle asked.

The Old man hesitated. He shrugged. "We're inside one of those grains of sand on the beach over there. We are floating on a breeze, at the bottom of an endless ocean."

"I'm not leaving until you stop taking the tunnel apart," Kyle said.

"Perseverance is an overrated human skill," the Old Man said, walking up the grassy hill to where Kyle had seen him before. "I'm not going to be able to help you, but sit if you must."

For the first time, from the hillside, Kyle could see the entire operation at once. The tunnel stretched beyond where Kyle could see on his right. The trench, which presumably used to hold part of the tunnel, stretched as far as Kyle could see to the left. Although the beach setting, with the purple, sunless sky beyond, was beautiful, Kyle sensed that the people were miserable.

The Old Man sat up. "I was expecting that if anyone found their way through, it would be Demetrius, the last Sere heir."

"He's been dead for years," Kyle said.

"I certainly hope not," the Old Man said through laughter. "He hasn't been born yet."

It took having the conversation a second time for Kyle to realize that Demetrius must be Kyle and Allaire's unborn baby. The name made perfect sense. He was Allaire's closest friend.

"So, the world will end when the tunnel is gone?" Kyle asked.

"The word 'end' is a human creation," the Old Man answered. "This word means nothing to me. Have we even started? I can't answer that either."

"Are you God?" Kyle asked.

The Old Man smiled. He looked at Kyle as if he were carefully considering his words. "I don't know."

Kyle had to resist trying to take everything he was experiencing in as a whole and instead focus on what was in front of him. "What did we do to deserve the world ending?"

"End. There's that word again. You're myopic," the Old Man answered. "You can't help it . . . Do you know who the last people were to break through from your side to mine?"

Kyle shook his head. What he didn't know could fill up the endless trench below.

"It was Simyon, and his brother, Umar, who became the first of your people," the Old Man said. "And ever since, Simyon's people have had to pay off the debt I levied on him for coming here in the first place."

"These people are miserable," Kyle said. "I can see it! Can't you?"

"They're paying a debt," the Old Man answered. "There's a necessary order to things. All is as it should be."

"When are they free of this debt?" Kyle asked.

"When your tunnel is gone," the Old Man answered.

"There has to be something else," Kyle said. "Something I can do, so you'll stop taking the tunnel apart."

The Old Man shook his head. "I'm afraid not. The betrayals have been too great."

"What betrayals?" Kyle asked. "Let me make this right."

"You can't," the Old Man said. "Your people

had one job. Keep the tunnel clear, so *this* wouldn't ever happen. When Simyon and his brother found the bridge between our two sides, I realized it could never be closed, so I gave Umar access to the entire timestream, to make sure he had the means to protect the vulnerability. And I gave him the special wood made from those Emphestus trees up there, in case he needed to return. That paddle you have with you is the only key he took to your side. I had Simyon's descendants build the Seres a portal to navigate time *only* if they needed to in order to protect the bridge between our worlds."

"The tunnel," Kyle said.

The Old Man nodded. "But, the temptation is too great. Time after time, the Seres have proven incapable of *not* using the tunnel for whatever *they* considered to be an exception to my rule."

"So, the reason for protecting the timestream has nothing to do with disturbing *time*, or changing the past?" Kyle asked. "It's all just to protect this? To protect you?"

"I'm important to protect," the Old Man said with a smile. "And, so is this place. Every time someone went into the tunnel, even with good intentions, they risked getting through. There can't be a bridge between our worlds, Kyle. You coming here only reaffirms why I'm getting rid of the tunnel."

"And then my world ends," Kyle said.

"Your world becomes part of the past," the Old Man said.

Kyle shook his head. "No. There has to be something I can do . . . If you didn't care why people were using the tunnel, why cause all of the earthquakes, or make things end up worse every time I tried changing the past?" Kyle asked.

"I've never been overly interested in what your people do with themselves," the Old Man said. "Free will is valuable . . . My job was just to do whatever I could to dissuade your people from using the tunnel. I would've done more if I could, but there are limitations, even for me."

Kyle couldn't believe his ears. What the Old Man was saying meant that everything Kyle and Allaire had thought about why the tunnel was shrinking was wrong. Ayers, for every horrible thing he'd done—and everything horrible he *hadn't* done because of Kyle and Allaire—hadn't been any more responsible for the tunnel shrinking than they had. In a way, Yalé had been correct.

"So, every time we went into the tunnel, even if it was to stop him, was just as bad as when Ayers went inside?" Kyle asked.

"Free will isn't the easiest thing to rein in," the Old Man answered. "Especially the desire to do something good."

"You said the Seres could never resist the temptation to use the tunnel," Kyle said.

"And I understand it," the Old Man answered. "I really do, Kyle. What a fantastic thought to be able to go back and *fix* whatever's broken. Especially for people who see things in black and white. Your efforts are admirable, Kyle. But, what's being undertaken now is necessary."

"Why is it necessary? Why is ending the world necessary?" Kyle asked, frustrated with the lack of answers. "Do you *know* what you'd be destroying?"

"Go back and enjoy your son," the Old Man said. "It'll take a while longer to dismantle the entire tunnel. And remember, if something *was* than it cannot end. It always exists in the past."

"It doesn't have to be in the past. We *can* resist," Kyle said. "Let me show you."

"It's too late," the Old Man said again.

Kyle turned toward the Old Man. "My world . . . My *side* . . . It's a pretty incredible place. I've been disappointed by people, but I've seen some pretty amazing things, too. Please. Please tell me how I can make this okay? I know you can stop this if you want to."

"You've been asking how you can make things okay for your entire life, Kyle," the Old Man answered. "And, you've gotten more chances than most people."

"I'll show you that we *are* capable of restraint," Kyle said. "I can't make up for what generations of Seres have done. All I can do is show you that I'm willing to make the sacrifice you wanted all of the Seres to make. Let me fix this. Let me show you there's a way to solve your problem without destroying my entire world."

The Old Man shook his head. "You've *already* done as much damage as any of your ancestors. I was glad to see Ayers go, but do you have any idea how many times you and Allaire entered the tunnel to make that happen? Like I said, there are things beyond even my control, Kyle."

"I don't believe that," Kyle said. "If I can go back and undo the damage I've done, and make sure no one can find their way back here ever again, what reason do you have to continue pulling the tunnel apart?"

"I really wouldn't bother," the Old Man said, his face tightening just a hint.

"But, *I would*," Kyle answered. "Just watch me. Before you doom my entire world . . . Promise me you'll watch."

The Old Man shrugged. "I can't help but watch."

"You'll see," Kyle said as he stood up. "We can resist." He ran quickly down the hill. Kyle knew he wasn't going to get any assurances from the Old Man, but he hadn't said "no" either.

When Kyle reached the trench, he saw the workers removing the top section of one part of the tunnel. As he was about to jump down into the trench and walk inside the roofless section of tunnel, Rosalee came up and stood beside him.

"Did you get what you came for?" she asked.

Kyle looked back up at the hill. Even from a distance, Kyle could tell that the Old Man was looking right at him. "I'm not sure, but I think so . . ."

"Will you be back?" she asked him.

"No," Kyle answered. "I don't think so."

"Can I come with you?" Rosalee asked. Kyle looked at her. They were the saddest eyes he'd ever seen, especially now. They were the eyes of someone who knew they were missing out on everything they wanted. He wondered if everyone here had such a keen sense of how empty and small their world was, or if she was somehow more acutely aware.

Kyle considered pulling her into the tunnel with him. He didn't know if he could save his world, but he might be able to save Rosalee from this one. "Have any of your people ever escaped?"

"They say we'd burn up if we tried," she answered.

"Then why do you want to come with me?" Kyle asked.

"We don't die here," Rosalee answered. "One day, you just stop getting older, and then you live in that body forever. I'd rather take my chances in there. But, if I survived, I'd have nowhere to go. I've never been off this beach."

"There's too much at stake," Kyle said, looking back at the Old Man again.

Rosalee shuffled her feet nervously. "Did he say what he's going to do with us once the tunnel is gone?"

"No . . . I'm sorry," Kyle said. "If I can do what I need to, maybe the tunnel won't ever go away . . . I'm not sure if that's a consolation or not, but—"

Rosalee nodded. "I'm sorry to even—"

"Don't be sorry," Kyle said. "I would if I could, but I have billions of people depending on me. And changing the Old Man's mind isn't going to be easy . . . " Her eyes looked sadder than ever, resigned to her fate. "You know, maybe at some point—"

"Good luck, Kyle," Rosalee said, lowering her head. She rubbed Kyle's shoulder gently and moved away from him.

Kyle nodded, but couldn't bear to look at Rosalee's face again. He jumped down into the trench and walked inside the tunnel. The purple light from the outside quickly dissipated and Kyle found himself in the familiar darkness in no time.

He climbed toward 2017. Fifteen minutes later, it was the first year he reached, meaning it was now the last accessible year in the tunnel.

CHAPTER 5

DECEMBER 27, 2017

eight months after kyle departed

KYLE WAS CONCERNED WHEN HE RETURNED TO THE factory building that it sounded too quiet, like it used to. There was no one in the main room, which was still decorated warmly with Yolanda's deft touch. Sillow's wife, and their daughters, Tinsley and Larkin, brought a feeling of hope and life to the factory. It felt like a home now, more than the sterile environment Kyle had grown used to during Yalé's time.

Kyle had a sense that time had passed, which was confirmed for him when he spotted his half-sister Tinsley, much taller than he remembered her, at the end of the hallway leading to the living quarters.

"Hey there," he called out.

She put her finger to her lips to shush him, and waved him over to her.

"Hi," he said. "Where is everyone?"

Still not saying a word, Tinsley turned and led him into the former gymnasium, where he found Sillow, Yolanda and his other half-sister, Larkin.

"Where's Allaire?" Kyle asked Sillow.

Sillow gestured for Kyle to sit beside him on the floor.

"Where is she?" Kyle asked. "Is something wrong?"

Again, Sillow gestured for Kyle to sit.

"Just tell me!" Kyle snapped, plopping himself down next to Sillow.

"She's fine," he whispered. "The baby's finally sleeping, so we're not making any noise right now."

"The baby?! How long has it been?" Kyle asked.

"It's been more than eight months," Sillow answered. "You have a beautiful baby boy."

Yolanda rubbed Kyle's back. "She named him Demetrius, and he's beautiful."

Kyle teared up immediately. He had missed nearly all of Allaire's pregnancy, and he'd missed the birth too. He wondered if it was the Old Man's doing. Kyle wondered if he was the one who controlled what day Kyle exited the tunnel.

"The baby was born early," Yolanda said. "He was totally fine, but another couple of weeks would've been ideal. Little guy wanted to get out into the world, though. They had her on bed rest since six months, so it was a blessing that he only arrived about a month ahead of schedule."

"And how's she doing now?" Kyle asked.

"She's doing okay. She misses you," Sillow said. "And neither of them are sleeping well."

Kyle had to resist the urge to go see her right then. He couldn't believe he'd missed almost the entire difficult pregnancy.

"She's really okay?" he asked.

Both Yolanda and Sillow nodded, and Kyle was able to take a deep breath again.

"Where did you go?" Sillow asked. "You went to check on the tunnel, and all of a sudden you're gone."

"It wasn't an easy pregnancy for her," Yolanda said. "I'm sure you had your reasons."

Kyle stood up and gestured to Sillow. "Let's go talk."

Yolanda rolled her eyes. "Sere business," she said to the girls.

"I'm sorry," Kyle said. Everything had changed, and Kyle owed it to Sillow to explain it to him first and let him decide how to tell his family.

"Yolanda, please let me know as soon as they're awake," Kyle said. "I want to meet my son."

A few minutes later, Kyle sat across from Sillow's desk. Sillow still had many of Yalé's documents hanging from the wall in an effort to understand the great mystery of their lives. Kyle couldn't help but smile now that he understood so much more.

"You've done an incredible job here," Kyle said to his father.

Sillow looked at the wall. "I've figured out a few more things since you left. Like, the paddle. It's a list of names—"

"I know," Kyle said.

"Where did you go?" Sillow asked.

"I know why all of this is happening," Kyle said. "It's not because we've been changing things in the timestream. It's because we've been using the tunnel at all."

Sillow looked at everything on his wall. "I don't understand. I've been doing calculations . . . I've identified a few points in history where perhaps something has been changed that shouldn't have."

"You've sunk yourself into this, Dad," Kyle said, feeling a bit like he was firing Sillow from a job he'd never actually applied for. "It's beyond impressive."

"Kyle, you need to understand something," Sillow said. "I did something terrible when you were young . . . "

"I know, Dad," Kyle said. "You've apologized for leaving, and I've forgiven you. It's not necessary to bring that up again."

"No," Sillow said. "There's something else. It's the reason I ran."

Kyle nodded, waiting. But, if he was being honest, he didn't know if he wanted to hear this. Kyle's relationship with Sillow was nearly repaired. Sillow had come through for Kyle on several occasions and now he had uprooted his life to live in the factory and take on Yalé's role. Kyle selfishly thought to himself that he didn't want anything complicating what he had to tell his father.

"Your mother," Sillow said. "I married her very young . . . I knew she was emotional, knew she could get depressed sometimes. But after we had you, it got really bad. It was hard to be around her. She'd cry at nothing. She'd get angry with me for no reason. The first year of your life was joyful in some ways, but miserable between me and your mother."

Kyle hadn't heard this take on the story of his father leaving before.

"None of it excuses what I did," Sillow said. "I'm just trying to explain how it happened."

"I understand, Dad," Kyle said. "But, it's not necessary."

"One night, I was out with some buddies after a job . . . This was back when I was doing some shady stuff," Sillow said. "And I called your mom from a pay phone to check on the two of you . . . She was hysterical like she always was then. She told me she thought she was going to hurt herself."

Kyle wasn't surprised to hear this. In a long-gone timestream, Kyle's mother had committed suicide shortly after Kyle was sentenced to his original prison sentence after the bus crash.

"That was it for me," Sillow continued. "I didn't believe she'd actually do anything, and I bailed.

Never came back again. I had some money from the job I'd just done and I couldn't get to Florida fast enough. Didn't even check back to make sure she was okay."

Kyle didn't know what to say. He couldn't tell his father what he'd done was okay. But, he'd long since forgiven him. His mother hadn't killed herself that night, of course.

"I was always a lost cause," Sillow said, "until you came back to me. You thought you needed me, but getting a second chance to do something for you saved me, Kyle. It let me be a better father to the girls than I ever was to you. I put my old life behind me . . . And then getting to come here and live with you, and figure all of this out, and learning that we're part of this ancient thing . . . I had something to prove to myself, and you let me do that . . . It's been a gift that I never deserved."

"Dad, it's a false gift," Kyle said. "Everything we've been doing has been wrong. It's the reason the world is going to end." Kyle hadn't expected a tearful discussion with his father. "Dad, you're making it so hard to tell you this, but the answer is so much simpler than any of us thought it was. The things we've done, they don't matter. We just weren't supposed to use the tunnel. That's it. Everything we've seen—the earthquakes, the tunnel shrinking, even heads exploding when someone sees another version of themselves—it's all just there to stop us from using the tunnel. But the Seres never got it, and now, our whole world is in big trouble."

"Then, what do we do?" Sillow asked.

"We end it," Kyle said.

"End it?" Sillow asked.

Kyle nodded. "That's right."

"What does that mean?" Sillow asked.

"You'll know when the time is right," Kyle said.

"What do you mean, *I'll know*?" Sillow asked. "I'm not like you. I don't have visions. The reason I've been doing all of this figuring is because I need something I can see. I'm not lucky like you."

"For now," Kyle said, "I just need you to shut down the machines. No more blots . . . I'll explain the rest later."

"But, what about the prophecy?" Sillow said, standing up and pointing to a page from a scroll Sillow had found in Yalé's papers. "It says if we stop spinning silk blots, the tunnel would close forever."

"It's not real," Kyle said. "Our ancestors lost the thread somehow. Maybe because, over time, the story got changed. And, maybe because they couldn't accept having such a unique ability and not being able to use it. But, all of the problems with the tunnel . . . All of the things that threaten the world now are because we've been using the silk blots in the first place."

"Can you fix it?" Sillow asked. "Can you save us?"

"I don't know," Kyle said. "But, I'm going to do the only thing that might help. I have something to prove too."

"Kyle," Yolanda said, appearing in the doorway of Sillow's office.

"Are they up?" Kyle asked, a huge smile curling on his face. He couldn't believe he was going to meet his son today.

"Yes, but you need to come quickly," Yolanda said. "There's something wrong."

CHAPTER 6

DECEMBER 27, 2017

seconds later

KYLE BURST INTO THE ROOM AND HIS EYES IMME-diately went to his son.

"He doesn't look good," Allaire screamed as she paced the room, holding the baby upright against her shoulder, bouncing him up and down quickly. "We need a doctor . . . C'mon Dee . . . C'mon . . . You're gonna be okay . . . Stay with me."

"Look at his color," Allaire continued despondently, tears rolling down her face. "He's fading away. We're losing him!"

Kyle was assaulted by nearly every sense. Here was his son in pajamas covered with vomit. The boy looked listless, his eyes glassy and lost.

"Yolanda's on the phone with nine-one-one," Sillow called into the room. "They're on the way."

Here was Allaire, more exhausted, and more upset, than he'd ever seen her. The sharp edges she usually created with her hair and makeup were nowhere to be found. "Tell them we don't have any time!"

Kyle reached his arms out to her. "Let me take him."

Allaire hesitated for a second.

Yolanda ran into the room. "They're on their way. They said to do CPR if we can't find a heartbeat."

Allaire started to bring her ear to Demetrius's chest and then stopped. She held him out, like she was presenting him to Kyle. "Can you?"

Kyle bent his ear to the baby's chest, and smiled. "There's a heartbeat! Let me try something."

Again, Allaire hesitated. "Oh, no. He doesn't look good!"

"Please," Kyle said, and Allaire finally handed Demetrius to him. "What happened?"

"I don't know," Allaire said, trying to form words as she sobbed. "He woke up screaming and covered in vomit. I picked him up and he started losing his color. And now he's like this, a lump of clay . . . "

Kyle saw the baby losing color and wracked his brain. He'd always thought of himself as being terrible in a crisis, one of those people whose brain went beyond foggy when his adrenaline kicked in. But since he'd first gone inside a silk blot, Kyle had learned to manage his nerves. He looked at his baby, quite possibly hanging onto life by a thread, and Kyle felt the world slow down. His thinking was clearer than ever, despite how hard his heart was pounding.

"What about the tunnel?" Allaire said. "Go back and warn me to wake him earlier."

Kyle considered the silk blot in his pocket and how he'd promised the Old Man he was capable of resisting using the tunnel to go back and change the past. *Could this entire moment have been manufactured to test Kyle?* he wondered. There wasn't much time.

"Wait," Kyle said, an idea springing into his head. He ran into the bathroom with Demetrius. Allaire followed right behind them.

If this didn't work, Kyle knew he'd go back into the silk blot to save the baby. It wasn't even a choice. Whatever the consequence, Kyle was not strong enough to let his newborn die. He couldn't live with being someone who could pass that test.

"Do something!" Allaire screamed.

Kyle turned on the faucet. He cupped his hands and started throwing cold water on the baby.

"What are you doing?" Allaire asked.

The cold surprise startled the baby, and he shuddered. It was the most Kyle had seen him move.

"What are you doing?" Allaire screamed again. "Get into the silk blot and fix this!" Even in the midst of this emergency, Kyle couldn't help but hear the Old Man's voice in his head. *The temptation is too great.*

Kyle threw another handful of water at Demetrius's face, and he coughed. A string of vomit escaped from the baby's mouth and onto his chin. Then, another cough, and more vomit. Within seconds, he started to cry. As he did, the red returned to his face, and Kyle saw the baby the way Allaire had gotten to know him over the past week. Kyle felt like he was going to be okay.

Allaire gently took the baby from Kyle and just looked at Demetrius for more than a minute. Even when Kyle pulled him back into his own arms, she didn't dare pull her eyes away now that he was showing such signs of improvement. Kyle looked at his son, examining every last centimeter of his face.

Kyle tried to memorize his face so he could recall it later. It was the little creature in his arms who would make him brave as he faced something he never thought he would again.

Kyle was sure that the choking incident had

been the Old Man's doing. A warning shot. If Kyle didn't hold up his end of the bargain—by making his sacrifice—then the Old Man would follow through with what he'd already started. The great test had begun.

Kyle handed the baby back to Allaire, and then moved behind her to squeeze her shoulders.

"Where *were* you all these months?" she whispered to him, still not taking her eyes off of Demetrius. "Didn't having a deadbeat father teach you anything?"

"Allaire, that's not fair," Kyle said. He thought about whether he had the fortitude to save the seven billion people on Earth when he had been so ready to forego his plan the moment his son was under duress.

"What's not fair is you disappearing," she said.

Demetrius bounced back even before the emergency medics made it to the factory. They still gave him a tiny oxygen mask for a few minutes, but the kid looked like a healthy baby again by then.

"You *live* here?" one of the medics asked Kyle.

"It's zoned for live-work," Kyle answered, knowingly lying to the EMT.

By the time the EMTs and firefighters cleared out, everyone in the factory was ready for bed. Kyle had planned to tell Allaire everything tonight—to tell her everything that he needed to do, even the things she might hate him for.

Instead, Kyle quickly passed out next to Allaire, who kept Demetrius in a bassinet next to the bed. Kyle had just met his son, and then nearly lost him. He hadn't even gotten a chance to tell Allaire where he'd been, and what he'd seen.

When Demetrius woke later that night, Allaire sat up to give him a feeding.

Kyle stirred, then sat up too and held his hands out to her. "Is there a bottle I can give him?"

Allaire handed Demetrius to Kyle and then grabbed a bottle from the kitchen. "I'm sorry about before. I was still shaken up . . . I'm really glad you're back. I've missed you." She shimmied forward and kissed him. She smiled when she pulled away. "*So* glad you're back." Then, she turned away and fell asleep almost instantly.

Kyle fed Demetrius until the baby fell back to sleep, and then held him a while longer. He had Kyle's ears, but his face was shaped like Allaire's. *What other qualities will he share with me as he grows up?* Kyle wondered. It ate at Kyle's core that he'd never get to find out. But tonight had only reinforced to Kyle what he must do. The thought of it made his entire body tense up for a moment.

Kyle had claimed he could break the generations-old inability of the Seres to resist using the tunnel, and if the Old Man was behind this, he'd done everything tonight except asking Kyle to actually prove it. The odds of Kyle randomly coming back through the silk blot to *this* evening were beyond unlikely.

He'd promised to break the chain of Seres who could not resist using the tunnel to try to change the course of their lives. Now, he just needed the Old Man to let him do that.

Kyle couldn't bear the thought of saying good-bye just yet, so he just held Demetrius for a while before going to sleep himself. Lying next to Allaire, he took in her familiar, intoxicating scent. He wasn't ready just yet, but he'd have to go soon. Tomorrow, there wouldn't be a choice. But for a few hours tonight, he pretended that they could just live like this forever.

CHAPTER 7

DECEMBER 27, 2017

later

THE OLD MAN'S FACE WAS SO CLOSE TO KYLE'S THAT he couldn't see anything past him.

"You're wrong," the Old Man said, with his arrogant laugh. "You really haven't learned a thing."

Kyle shook his head angrily. "You're not real!"

The Old Man shrugged and smiled. "Are you really in any position to say something like that these days, Kyle? How do you know what's real anymore?"

Kyle felt a hand on his shoulder, but when he looked down, he realized the Old Man's body wasn't there. His head was just floating right in front of Kyle's face.

He heard crying, but when Kyle brought his hand to his own face, there were no tears.

The Old Man's head rose into the air and hung there for a second, before flying off through the ceiling like a balloon heading skyward. Before he even lost sight of the Old Man, another disembodied head floated into Kyle's view. Again, it was only an inch or two away from Kyle's own face. It was his old cellmate and friend, Ochoa.

Ochoa shook his head, and his long, black curly hair moved side to side. "You ain't right, bro . . . Just think about it."

"No!" Kyle said. "You're dead. You're not here."

Ochoa hissed through his teeth. "Yo, just think about it. Your whole plan is off, bro."

Again, Kyle shook his head hard. There was the feeling of a hand on his shoulder again, but it wasn't Ochoa's either.

Ochoa's head started floating toward the ceiling too, but then it slowly fell toward Kyle again. "One more thing. You didn't ever think to go back and try to save my ass, bro? Thanks for nothin'."

Now, Ochoa's head popped apart, just like it had

in Washington Heights on Kyle's first trip through time. Ochoa had seen the younger version of himself and paid the price with his life. Instead of brains and blood this time, the remnants of his head just faded into thin air.

Kyle's mother's head appeared with more of a neck than the other two. And her neck, of course, had the deep red bruising from the clothesline she'd used to hang herself during Kyle's prison sentence.

"I'm so sorry, Mom," Kyle said.

Kyle's mom shook her head. She didn't want to hear his words. She just looked deep into Kyle's eyes and shook her head, as if her neck were squarely attached to a body.

"I don't understand, Mom," Kyle said, shaking his head as well.

Now, he felt hands on both shoulders.

Kyle's mom just shook her head "no" over and over, as her head floated toward the ceiling.

Kyle wanted it to stop, but he had no control.

Now, Young Ayers took the same place as the other heads in front of Kyle.

"I didn't die so you could mess this up, Mr. Kyle," he said.

"What do you mean?" Kyle screamed. "Just tell me what I'm doing wrong!" Kyle felt a hand over his mouth now. He tried to keep talking, but the sound of his own voice was muffled to him.

"Think about it," Young Ayers said.

Kyle tried speaking again, but couldn't. His mouth felt like it didn't work. His lips smothered so tightly, he couldn't form words.

Suddenly, behind Young Ayers's head, the twelve faces of the children of Bus #17 floated into view, along with his best friend, Joe Stropoli, and the bus driver, Bruno.

"It's not that hard to figure out," Scarlett Finch, one of the seventh graders, said.

Lisa Cartigliani, who'd blown up the high school after Kyle finally managed to stop the bus crash, laughed hysterically before catching her breath. "Just keep doing what you're doing, asshole."

Marlon Peters looked at Kyle with his soulful eyes and shook his head. "I forgive you . . . Is that what you need?"

Etan Rachnowitz floated in front of Marlon's face. "You don't know shit, you butt-sniffing turd eater. You're gonna fuck this up like you fuck up everything."

The faces continued to linger for what felt like several minutes. Kyle's guilt from the bus crash that ruined his simple high school existence rushed back to him. It had never really subsided, if Kyle was being honest. He'd just gotten distracted with everything else he'd discovered while time weaving.

All at once, the faces from the day of the crash faded away and baby Demetrius's head took their place. His week-old infant son just screamed and screamed but somehow Kyle knew he was trying to say the same thing everyone else was. Finally, instead of resisting, Kyle finally considered what it was that he wasn't getting . . . ? What was he missing? He'd promised *to show the Old Man that he could resist altering his own fate in exchange for leaving the tunnel—and by extension, mankind—alone. And what Kyle planned to do would undoubtedly accomplish that. What else was there to consider?*

Kyle tried to speak to his son. He was surprised when he could move his mouth again. "I'm sorry," he said, trying to speak loudly over the wail of Demetrius's screams.

Suddenly, the room started to shake, but it wasn't like the earthquakes Kyle had experienced since he started time weaving. It was more like being on a boat. Or like someone was shaking him by the shoulders.

Kyle opened his eyes and saw Allaire's face in front of his. He looked down and her body was attached. As he reached up and touched her shoulders, he realized her hands were on his upper arms, gently shaking him. "It's okay, Kyle. You're safe here. You're home," she said over the screams of Demetrius, lying in his bassinet next to the bed.

"You had a bad dream. And the baby's hungry again. This kid is *not* shy when it comes to eating."

Kyle was still shaken up. He couldn't get the idea out of his head that there was some flaw in his plan—something that would prevent him from proving to the Old Man that it was possible to resist the tunnel. And that it was possible to turn your back on the life you desperately want, and the people you desperately want to hold.

As Kyle lay in bed, too jarred by his dream to sleep, but too exhausted to move, he watched Allaire feeding Demetrius. He stroked her forearm with his fingernails and kept stopping himself from starting the conversation he knew they needed to have.

Finally, just as his eyes began to close, his hand limply falling away from Allaire's arm, she moved Demetrius back to his bassinet and slid down in the bed so her face was next to Kyle's. The movement caused Kyle to open his eyes and he found her face, again, only inches from his.

He was about to tell her what he had to do.

He knew it would shock her to hear that he was planning to go back to the day of the bus crash. He looked Allaire in the eyes, and knew he couldn't wait any longer to tell her. She deserved to know that for all of her sacrifices for the Seres, she was going to have to make one more, and let Kyle go.

"Don't," she said. "I'm begging you."

"What?" Kyle asked.

"Don't leave us," she said.

Kyle started to speak again. He started to open his mouth to explain that there wasn't a choice. His eyes filled with tears. Before he could get a word out, though, she held her forefinger to his mouth. "Tomorrow, my love."

Kyle felt a huge sense of relief, which lasted up until he closed his eyes and thought about the fact that he and Allaire would never spend another night together again.

CHAPTER 8

DECEMBER 28, 2017

the next day

EARLY THE NEXT MORNING, KYLE HELD THE
wooden paddle in his hand while he paced around
the main factory room. There were silk blots just
hanging there, ready for anyone with the genetic
ability to survive the tunnel to use.

If the Seres had known that every single trip
into the tunnel had further cemented their fate,
and the fate of the world, he wondered how many
of his ancestors would've done anything differ-
ently. Clearly, over time, the message from the Old
Man had been lost. Whether it had been ignored,
deliberately misinterpreted, or simply improperly

communicated, was not something Kyle would ever know for sure.

Kyle wondered whether the Old Man would even see him again if he went back now. Kyle hadn't met his son yet when he volunteered to prove to the Old Man that he could rise above temptation. Kyle couldn't help but feel that this should be someone else's role to fill, now that he was a father. Kyle wondered how he could bring himself to leave his family, just as his own dead-beat father had done. Especially since what Kyle planned to do would leave no possibility of making up for lost time later. But Kyle knew it was his responsibility to ensure that there *was* a "later."

"We should talk," Allaire said, walking in so quietly that Kyle hadn't noticed her.

"Where's the baby?" Kyle asked.

Allaire smiled. "He's got you wrapped around his little finger already, huh?"

Kyle smiled without opening his mouth. Tears

weren't far away, and if he moved his facial muscles too much, he might lose it.

"Yolanda has him," Allaire continued. "He'll probably go down for a nap soon. He had a rough night of sleep."

"I'm sorry about making so much noise last night," Kyle said. "I had bad dreams."

"About leaving?" Allaire asked.

Kyle wondered how she knew. Even so, he hesitated to say it out loud, because then it would be real. He also couldn't understand why he had such a strong sense that his plan was somehow wrong. That he was missing something important. That there was some detail he'd neglected to consider.

"It's more than just leaving, Allaire," Kyle said.

Allaire had obviously been ready for this since last night, and her tone immediately got cold and angry. "What's *worse*, Kyle, than leaving your child?"

He needed to try to make her understand.

"Do you remember you said from now on,

we'd do everything together?" she continued. "No exceptions? So, tell me, what's worse than you leaving us?"

"I saw something, Allaire," he said. "While I was gone . . . I found a way to break through the tunnel."

"What?" she asked, her eyes widening.

"I tried drilling through with a diamond bit, and couldn't even make a dent," he said. "But I threw the wooden paddle and it cut through like the tunnel was made of cream cheese."

Kyle told Allaire about meeting Simyon and the Old Man, and about the clan of people taking the tunnel apart. He told her that the Old Man was taking the tunnel apart because the Seres had proven they couldn't resist the temptation to use the tunnel to change the history of their own lives, and the Old Man thought the risk of anyone breaking through was too great to keep it open.

"But you broke through, and nothing happened," Allaire said. "We're still here."

"I don't understand everything, Allaire," Kyle said. "No one could. But, this Old Man, he's going to end the world if I can't change his mind." Kyle grabbed Allaire's hand, wanting desperately for her to understand. "I begged him not to give up on humanity. I told him I was going to prove to him that we—"

"We?" Allaire said, cutting him off.

"We . . . The Seres . . . " Kyle said. "I told him I was going to prove that we could stop using the tunnel to solve our own problems. We were never supposed to go into the tunnel at all. Even to stop Ayers. We were making it worse, not better."

Kyle could see Allaire's face fall. So much of her life had been devoted to chasing Ayers.

"How long?" she asked, tears streaming down her face.

Kyle knew she knew, and didn't answer at first.

"Don't do it!" she said. "Just don't. How do you know this man will end the world if you just stay here? How do you know he even can? We can just stop using the tunnel. We'll blow up the factory. We can move far away."

"You knew it before I did," Kyle said. "Maybe you didn't understand the real reason why, but you knew from the start that changing the day of the bus crash was a mistake. It's how we met, Allaire!"

Allaire broke down and leaned against the smallest of the machines in the main factory room. Kyle put his arm around her and led her to their bedroom. She started speaking several times, but she couldn't get words out between her sobs. "So, what are you going to do?" she finally asked.

"The only way I can show him that I can resist using the tunnel to fix my own life is to go back and not fix it," Kyle said. "I need to make sure the bus crash happens, and that I never get into a silk blot in the first place."

"Why does it have to be you?" Allaire asked.

"That writing on this paddle?" Kyle answered. "It's a long list of names. Sere heirs going back thousands of years. And the last name on the paddle isn't mine. It's our son's. If I don't end this, he's going to have to, Allaire. And, I'd rather be a deadbeat than saddle him with that. Don't you want better for him than you had?"

Allaire kept starting to move her mouth. Kept shaking her head "no." Kyle could see she was desperately trying to find the words to change his mind, even if she knew he was right. "Are you sure? Are you even sure this is going to work?"

"No," Kyle answered. "But the Old Man didn't say *no* when I begged him for the chance."

"So that's it?" Allaire asked. "You come up with this plan. This guy on a hill doesn't agree—he just *doesn't say no*—and we never see you again? You're giving up a lot on a hunch, Kyle."

"If it weren't me," Kyle said. "If it were someone else, and they were taking a shot at saving the rest of humanity, and giving your son a life, what would you say?"

"I'm so stupid," Allaire said, shaking her head and looking off across the room. "I thought we'd have a baby and it would somehow make our lives normal. That we'd go to parks and farmer's markets, and change diapers. Finally, I was going to have something great."

"You will have that . . . with Demetrius," Kyle said. "But me? I don't get to have that."

Allaire rolled her eyes. "Why not, though?"

"I blew it, Allaire," Kyle said. "The price I paid was steep, but this timestream . . . this second chance? It was never mine to have forever. I'm just happy I got it for a little while."

Allaire blew the strands of hair from her face, something she'd been doing since she was the teenage girl Kyle first met. "Damn you, Kyle Cash." She leaned her head against him and balled her hands into fists, lightly tapping them on his chest. "Damn you."

Kyle could tell that she was done fighting, and he wrapped his arms around her. "You can't go looking for me," Kyle said. "And neither can Demetrius. Ever. No more time weaving.

By now, the fight was out of Allaire, and she nodded.

"Make sure he knows his father didn't leave him," Kyle said. "Please. And make sure he knows I had no choice."

"Will you stay a few more hours?" she asked softly.

Kyle nodded, and she tilted her head up to kiss his lips. Her face was warm and red. As they kissed, she pulled him on top of her. Kyle moved his hands down her body. He worried that this would only make it harder to leave, but realized immediately what a ridiculous thought that was. Getting into a silk blot in a few hours, leaving Allaire, Demetrius and his father, for the final time, was going to be the hardest thing he ever had to do. Nothing he and Allaire shared now could possibly make it harder, so he gave himself to the moment, enjoying every second. He tried hard to concentrate on how everything felt, so that later, he could summon the memories of their last day together.

CHAPTER 9

AS USUAL, KYLE EXITED THE SILK BLOT ON exactly the day he'd hoped to. It was early afternoon on the day before the bus crash—early enough for Kyle to catch his mother at her job, and most importantly, early enough to know that the 2014 version of himself was still at school.

He walked into Flairin' Edies, one of the two dry cleaning shops in Flemming, and saw his mother pulling an order from the giant conveyor belt of hanging clothing. She once told him that about a quarter of the orders on there were ones that were never picked up. Her boss thought it made the business look better to have the belt full, so the unclaimed clothing just stayed year after year, untouched artifacts of earlier fashions.

When his mother finished with her customer, she took off the reading glasses she used for reading the small print on the shop's computer screens. "Is it three o'clock already?"

"We got out early today, Mom," Kyle answered.

"Wait," she said, holding her hand up, and examining him closely. "You look different."

"I'm really tired, Mom," Kyle said. "That's probably why."

"Honey, what do you need?" she asked, still looking at him skeptically. "Hold on a sec and I'll grab my wallet from the back."

Kyle smiled. He hadn't known just how depressed she was before. And then, a few months after his sentencing, she killed herself. Now, he felt like he could sense the emptiness in her eyes. "I don't need money, Mom."

His mother cocked her eyebrows at him.

"Oh . . . Then, what do you need, honey? I'm at work."

"Can we talk, mom?" he asked.

"Uh, sure," she stammered. Kyle knew his old self enough to know that it was unusual for him to show up at his mom's job for no reason. She looked toward the back of the store, and stuck her hands between two hangers, making a gap on the conveyor belt. "Hey Marjorie, mind if I take a quick break? Sorry, I'll just be a minute."

A few seconds later, Kyle followed his mother outside the store. She leaned against the back of a bus stop bench, and shrugged her shoulders. "I hope this isn't bad news . . . You *really* look different. Did you get a haircut? It can't just be that. What's going on, Kyle?"

"It's not bad news," Kyle said. "Not right now, at least." He knew what he wanted his mother to do, or more accurately, *not* to do. But the words didn't come easily. They'd lived in the same house for Kyle's entire life before the crash, but as a teenager, Kyle realized that he'd barely talked to his mother about anything. He'd spent so much more time trying to evade her than relating to her.

"Spit it out, honey," his mom said. "What's going on? How bad could it be?"

"Mom," Kyle said. "Something's going to happen, and there's nothing I can do to stop it."

"What are you talking about?" she asked. "What *thing*? Are you in trouble, Kyle?"

Kyle shook his head. "Listen, Mom, there's nothing you or I can do. It's just . . . It's going to happen. But when it does, I need you to know something."

His mom took a deep breath. "I don't under—"

"Mom, just listen, please," he said. "A lot of people are going to look at what happens and say you have a good-for-nothing son. And, maybe they're right. But you need to know that, for once in his life, he did something right. What you're going to see isn't the whole story."

"How do you know all of this?" Ms. Cash asked. "Did your father get in touch or something?"

"Mom, I know you're sad," Kyle said.

"I'm fine, honey," she said.

Kyle shook his head. "You're not . . . I want you to be happy, but it's going to get even harder starting tomorrow. But you need to know that all of it is for the best. I wish it weren't. I wish I could change it all, but I . . . But, I know now it's not supposed to change."

His mom's eyes filled with tears now. "I don't understand why you're saying all of this. What's going to happen? Why are you telling me all of this?"

"Because you need to be strong," Kyle said. "Stronger than you think you can be. Strong enough to know that when everything is happening to me that it's for the best. And you need to not punish yourself."

"If you can't do anything about it, maybe I can?" she said, crying now. "Let me help you."

Kyle shook his head. "I'm serious. I don't care how depressed you get, you need to take care of yourself and not do anything crazy. I need you to take care of yourself," Kyle said. "And don't mention this conversation to me again. Please. Even after tomorrow. If you do, I'll just pretend I don't know what you're talking about."

She wiped her eyes. "I really don't understand you. Are you on drugs?"

"All you need to understand, Mom, is that everything that happens is exactly what *needs* to happen, even if you can't see it. There's a bigger picture here," Kyle said, choking back tears himself. "Promise me that you won't hurt yourself."

She nodded. "It sounds like you're in some kind of trouble. Please, let me help you. I'll tell Marjorie I'm sick. I can leave right now. Just give me thirty seconds. Let me help you."

Kyle hugged her. He knew it must have been years since he'd initiated a hug between them. "Go back to work, Mom. I love you. Remember, it's important we don't talk about this again, okay?"

She pulled away from the hug, and took him in with her eyes. She might feel skeptical and confused, but he thought he'd said enough to make her take him seriously. "Be careful," she said.

Kyle nodded. "Just don't give up on me, Mom," he said, and then quickly turned around before he started crying in front of her.

CHAPTER 10

OUTSIDE OF TIME

SIMYON CONSIDERED WALKING IN THE OTHER direction before Taio even reached him. The same way Simyon was the only one of his people to ever speak with the Old Man, his best friend was the unofficial designee to have any tough conversations with Simyon.

When Taio was determined, there was no putting him off, so Simyon knew any delay tactic he'd try would work only so well.

Taio reached him quickly, clearly in no mood to be leisurely about anything. "Everyone's scared," Taio said.

"I'm trying to get answers," Simyon said.

"I don't *see* you trying to get answers," Taio said. "You haven't gone to him since before the announcement."

The Old Man had breached his own protocols by gathering Simyon's entire tribe and announcing to all of them at once, his deep bellowing voice carrying loud and clear to the farthest reaches of the camp, that all work on the tunnel would be suspended for the time being.

"They want to know what 'suspended,' means," Taio said. "They're afraid this is the end."

"And what if it is?" Simyon asked, waving his hand in front of him dismissively. Was it his responsibility to manage everyone's emotions? Simyon thought to himself.

Taio's face tightened. Simyon was more honest with Taio than with anyone else, but he was never outright pessimistic. Even after the change from building the tunnel to taking it apart, Simyon had kept a brave face. But ever since the man from the other side had broken through the tunnel and gotten an audience with the Old Man, Simyon wondered if he was still the right man to lead his people. Leaders took action, and Simyon had never been allowed even the illusion of real power. All he did was manage the concerns of the larger group, and occasionally give them made up answers to keep from inciting panic.

"Do *you* think this is the end?" Taio asked.

"I don't know," Simyon answered.

"But what do you think?" Taio asked again.

Simyon nodded. "I think Kyle came from the other side, and he might've changed the Old Man's mind. I never imagined that happening. *I've* certainly never changed his mind about anything."

"What if we all go to him?" Taio asked. "What if all go to him and insist on answers?"

Simyon smiled. "He wouldn't like that."

"But what could he do?" Taio asked. "We could threaten to go into the tunnel."

"Remember what happened when the men went beyond the trees?" Simyon asked. "He told me he considered just getting rid all of us then. He said he could just make all of us, and the tunnel, disappear with the flick of his wrist. We can't push him, Taio."

"I promised everyone some answers," Taio said. "I don't know if we can hold them off much longer. Most of them already know they're never going to get to cross over. So, what do they have to lose if they think the Old Man is just going to get rid of us all anyway?"

"Give me a little while," Simyon said. "Let's see if this Kyle kid might've changed his mind."

Taio looked at him skeptically. "You really think that happened?"

Simyon shrugged. "If it did, it means we'll get to start rebuilding soon. And, building is endless . . . Being here without anything to do is what scares *me*."

Taio nodded. "So, I should tell them that we'll start building again soon?"

Simyon nodded. "Yes, I think you should say just that."

As Taio walked away, Simyon turned toward the hill and saw the Old Man sitting with his arm in the air—his signal for Simyon to approach. In the hundreds of generations that Simyon had known him, the Old Man had summoned him less than a dozen times. Simyon hoped he hadn't gotten wind of the idea of his people storming up the hill and demanding answers.

He walked slowly toward the grassy hillside, desperately hoping he'd have some actual good news to bring back to his people.

CHAPTER 11

MARCH 12, 2014

the night before the original bus crash

EVEN FOR A MAN WHO NORMALLY APPEARED A bit rough, Sillow looked terrible when he came out as he entered the baggage claim at John F. Kennedy airport in New York. He and Kyle locked eyes and Sillow looked away before doing a double-take and then heading toward his son.

"You told me to take the bus up to Flemming," Sillow said. "You said I wasn't even supposed to see you."

"Plans changed, Dad," Kyle said.

"How so?" Sillow asked, looking Kyle in the eyes. He'd gotten so used to the other Sillow that the aggressive posture was jarring to Kyle. "I've been planning to be here the last sixteen years. Has this been some kind of joke the whole time?"

Kyle shook his head. "Of course not. I'm not surprised you're here. We've done this before, and you come through for me every single time. Whatever you think about anything you've ever done, just know that."

Sillow moved closer to Kyle's face. "I don't need a fuckin' pep talk, kid."

Kyle pulled a piece of folded paper out of his back pocket and handed it to Sillow.

"The fuck?" Sillow asked as he looked at the plane ticket back to Florida. "I came all the way here."

Kyle wished his father would just turn around. He needed to summon every ounce of his own energy for what he had to do tomorrow, and he'd already had a meaningful goodbye with a version of his father who'd grown up and become someone Kyle not only loved, but liked.

It would be so easy for Kyle to go back to Allaire

in 2017 and just live out however much time the human race had left. The last thing he needed was Sillow making this any harder.

"I'm sorry," Kyle said. "You need to go back."

Sillow put the ticket into his pocket and shrugged. "Why should I trust you? Shit, you can time travel. How do I know someone can't just make another version of you or somethin'?"

"You believed me then," Kyle said. "Enough to get on that plane."

"The plane almost fuckin' crashed," Sillow said.

"Listen," Kyle said, "the bus crash needs to happen. I know that now."

Sillow smiled, as if he couldn't believe what he was hearing. "What about the twelve kids? That was quite a sob story, kid. You know how pissed my wife was that I was comin' here? Thinks I'm steppin' out or something . . . I'm not in the line of work where you get to take fancy business trips."

"I'm sorry, Dad," Kyle said. "Please get on this flight. It leaves in an hour."

CHAPTER 12

MARCH 13, 2014

the morning of the bus crash

KYLE HAD A GUN IN HIS BACKPACK, BUT HOPED he could get himself onto Bus #17 without any violence. He hid behind a tree on the bus driver's block. He had no idea what to expect. He hoped that if he could make the crash happen just as it originally had, except with one version of himself on the bus, and the other driving Joe's Audi, that it would prove to the Old Man that at least *he* could resist the temptation to use the tunnel to fix his life. It would leave this version of Kyle dead, and the other version of him exactly as he'd been the first time, in jail.

Of course, any number of things could go

wrong. If Kyle made the driver late, by even a few seconds, it could change the result of the crash, or even cause it not to happen at all. He needed to get on the bus without an ordeal.

"Mr. Pasquale," Kyle said. "I'm Jeff White. The company sent me to observe today's ride."

Bruno stopped and just looked at Kyle for a second. "What are you observing?"

"It's standard," Kyle said, conscious of the fact that this was already taking too long. "I'm just makin' the rounds. Gotta fill out a form that says I took the ride. Bureaucratic bullshit, if you ask me. Sorry for the surprise. They were supposed to give you a heads up yesterday."

Kyle knew his plan could be busted with a single phone call, or call over the bus's radio, but he had no choice but to take his chances.

Bruno stood there again. He had the look of a man who could separate bullshit from the genuine article and Kyle's heart started beating. If he accidentally stopped the bus crash from happening this time around, everything he hoped to accomplish would be in jeopardy.

"You won't even know I'm there," Kyle said, trying once more.

Bruno just looked at him and walked around the bus, climbing into the driver's seat. The engine roared on and Kyle reached for the gun at the back of his pants. If Bruno drove away without Kyle, the entire plan would be shot.

Just as Kyle was about to pull the gun and point it at Bruno through the window of the bus, the passenger door opened up.

"Thanks," Kyle said, climbing the two steps and taking the first seat behind Bruno as quickly as he could, laying his bag on the seat next to him. Taking in the bus's familiar interior, Kyle had the feeling again that he'd forgotten something again. He had trouble putting the thought out of his head that his plan had some kind of fatal flaw to it.

Kyle looked at the analog clock on Bruno's dashboard and saw it was 7:46. He knew the original bus crash took place at 8:59, but it was too early for Kyle to know whether they were running late. Originally, Kyle had felt the universe resisting every effort he made to prevent the bus crash, which he knew now was simply the Old Man's effort to dissuade anyone from entering the tunnel in the hopes of changing the past. But in the latest time-stream Kyle knew, the crash *hadn't* happened, so he wondered which direction the universe would push toward, or whether the Old Man might even try to influence the outcome himself, one way or the other.

When Kyle saw the clock pass 8:30, he counted five of the twelve kids already on the bus. Even though he'd been on the bus before, during his effort to stop the crash, it was still mind-blowing for Kyle to be surrounded by all of the children he'd killed in the crash. He knew that Marlon, sleeping against the window in the third row of seats, collected Dr. Seuss books, and still had the *Cat in the Hat* painted on the wall of his bedroom. And, he knew that Amelie Finch was the best player on her Little League softball team. Lisa Cartigliani, gossiping loudly with her best friend Tiffany across the two back seats, was the biggest mystery of all to him. Nothing he'd learned about her during all of his time trolling articles, recollections on her Facebook page, or anywhere else he could learn about her, pointed to someone violent enough to blow up a school.

The bus stopped, and Kyle turned when he felt a chilly breeze at his back.

Lisa was hanging halfway out the tiny opening of the lowered bus window. "Hey, bitch!" she yelled out to Etan Rachnowitz as he walked out of his house. He held his middle finger up at his friend, and then turned back to the front door where Kyle saw Myrna Rachnowitz standing, waving goodbye to her little brother. Myrna was the person who'd first drawn Kyle into the crazy existence he inhabited now.

He looked at her and wondered about the truth. Was she Ayers's lover, as Yalé claimed? Knowing what Kyle knew now, he doubted it. Yalé had told Kyle that Ayers set up the entire scenario of Kyle time weaving to change the crash in order to convince Myrna to marry Ayers. But, Kyle knew that Ayers never wanted to settle down and carry on the Seres' tradition at the factory. It made more sense that Ayers had simply used her to approach Kyle because it would be more believable if a family member of one of the crash victims came to propose the idea to Kyle. It made more sense to Kyle that Ayers had been pulling strings from the very beginning, leading to their first meeting at the Silo when Ayers asked Kyle to "never" with him. Kyle knew now that he'd never get the chance to learn every last detail about what led him here.

Kyle watched Myrna wave goodbye to her

brother, hoping it was for the final time, as the bus drove up the street toward its next stop.

The ride continued along without any perceptible problems until they pulled in front of Patty Marshall's apartment building.

When he didn't see her standing in front of the three-story building, Bruno honked the horn and sat on it for ten or fifteen seconds.

Kyle had stopped worrying about the crash's timeline as the entire morning pickup had gone off without a hitch so far, and for all he knew, Patty had been late to come downstairs on the morning of the original crash too.

"Hey, Jeff," Bruno called out, as Kyle stared out at the front of Patty's building, hoping she'd walk through the front door any second. "Hey, Jeff?" Kyle just stared at the door. "Jeff! Hey!"

Jeff? Kyle thought to himself. *There was no Jeff*

on Bus #17. When Kyle turned to Bruno, he saw the driver looking at him like he was crazy.

"You forget your own name?" Bruno asked him.

"Sorry," Kyle said. "I'm sorry."

"Make yourself useful," Bruno said in his thick accent, opening the passenger door up. "Go buzz up to apartment 3C and tell them the bus is here for Patricia. Sometimes they forget to call when they get sick. Stupid parents."

Kyle nodded at him, got up and exited the bus. He walked as fast as he could, conscious of the fact that he was not part of the original morning of the crash—not *this* part.

He pressed the buzzer labeled "Marshall" and waited.

As he pressed the button again a few seconds later, he saw that Bruno was on the bus's radio. Kyle wondered if not responding to his fake name had made Bruno suspicious enough to check out his story with the bus company. Kyle saw Bruno shaking his head as he talked into the radio.

Kyle pushed the buzzer once more.

As he stood, no longer expecting an answer through the speaker, he saw Bruno get out of his seat and exit the bus through the passenger side.

Kyle began to panic and suddenly regretted the risky back story he'd given to the elderly Italian immigrant. If Bruno figured out that Kyle wasn't an observer from the bus company, he certainly wasn't going to let him back on the bus. Worse, any confrontation they had would make the bus later and later to Banditt Drawbridge, increasing the chances of the bus crash never happening at all.

Just as Bruno got within a few feet of him, a voice came from the speaker on the buzzer panel. "Yeah?" the voice said, crackly, but meek.

"Hi, uh, yeah," Kyle said. "The bus is outside for Patty."

"No one called you?" the voice asked.

"I'm sorry?" Kyle said, his heart sinking. If Patty was out sick from school, she wouldn't be on the bus when it crashed, which meant there was no way the original twelve kids would be killed in the crash. Kyle knew that small changes could lead to bigger ones.

"She died this weekend," the voice said, and Kyle felt guilty to be relieved.

By now, Bruno was standing next to Kyle. "We're sorry to bother you," Bruno said, leaning in front of Kyle. "Very sorry for your loss."

Kyle was shaken by the news Patty was already dead. *Would the crash even happen now?* he wondered, *without all of the original children on the bus?*

The bus pulled up to the last house on their morning route at 8:59, the time of the original bus crash. Kyle tried not to panic, since the second time the crash happened—after his first attempt to stop it—the collision took place a few minutes later. Again, Kyle had the thought that he'd forgotten something.

Like he'd missed some key detail. Since he couldn't figure out what it was, he tried to put the thought out of his head.

Paul Hacker's mom walked out to the bus with him, wearing the same Lululemon yoga pants that every mom in Flemming wore.

"I apologize," Bruno called out to her, as he opened the door.

"They're not supposed to be late," Paul's mom said, as she nudged her son onto the bus. "Don't let this happen again, please," she said. "I'm on the school board, you know?"

"Something bad happened," Bruno answered, shaking his head. "One of the children passed away."

As Paul's mom tripped over her words, trying to ask for details at the same time as she apologized to Bruno, he just closed the door and pulled away. At the end of the block, though, Bruno stopped the bus and pulled to the side.

The bus was quieter with eleven students

onboard than it had been with only two or three. Once the children heard over the bus's radio that Patty had died, they'd barely spoken more than whispers to each other for the rest of the ride. Kyle could see that Bruno was shaken up too.

"Hey, Jeff," Bruno said, standing up from the driver's seat.

This time, Kyle was on it and looked up right away.

"Would you mind driving for a few minutes?" Bruno asked. "I can't believe it about the girl . . . I picked her up Friday. She was fine."

Kyle stood up and froze for a few seconds. He started shaking and wondered whether this was a test from the Old Man again, or whether the circumstances of this morning were just different enough to lead to this. Without saying anything, Kyle took the driver's seat and tried to calm his hands so he could grip the steering wheel. There was no way Bruno could know what he was asking of Kyle.

Now, the crash might be completely in Kyle's hands. If the timing of this morning's pickups, and stopping at Patty's apartment building hadn't made the crash an impossibility, it would have to be Kyle now who let the bus collide with Joe Stropoli's Audi, also driven by Kyle, when he was two years younger.

Before pressing his foot down on the gas, Kyle wondered if he'd be able to do it. *Can I make the crash happen myself?* he wondered. He thought about Lisa Cartigliani, sitting in the back, quiet, he imagined, for once, because she was shell-shocked from the news about Patty. If she lived through today, there was a good chance history would repeat itself in this new timestream and she would kill hundreds at Silverman High School the following school year when she rigged the entire building with explosives. Kyle had never thought about it before, but wondered if she had help, or if she was framed. *Did Ayers have a hand in blowing up the high school?* Kyle wondered. *Or did the Old Man, in order to dissuade Kyle from time weaving again?*

Kyle hit the gas to gather speed for one of the huge hills on Nairn Boulevard, and seconds later, the bus began its climb. The vehicle chug-chugged slowly, but admirably, given the weight of the school bus. Kyle took in the view, likely for the last time, from the top of the hill. He and Joe had come the other way, driving down the Nairn Boulevard's other huge hill, so many times, so carefree. Now, the fact that he was about to die really hit Kyle. While the Kyle of this timestream would live, and go to prison, *this* Kyle would simply be gone—an aberration created by time weaving finally corrected.

Almost worse, though, was the fact that he was in complete control of it. He could swerve the bus out of the way. He could turn into the housing development at the bottom of the hill and miss passing the Audi completely.

But, Kyle reminded himself, *I didn't come here*

to change my mind. And I didn't come to save Kyle Cash. I came to kill him.

The bus rolled fast down the slick hill, straight toward Banditt Drawbridge. Kyle could barely appreciate one more chance to see the familiar sight of his hometown as it rushed past in a blur. At the bottom of the hill on the bus's left was Silverman High. To the right there were rolling hills covered by a couple of adjoining high-end housing developments and a 7-Eleven. Kyle took his foot off the gas as the bus flew down the hill.

He spotted Joe's Audi coming down the hill on the other side of the drawbridge and felt a combination of relief and sadness. The children of Bus #17 didn't deserve to die, they never had. But, on the original morning of the crash, and each of the other times it happened, the kids had drawn the terrible luck to share Banditt Drawbridge with the car Kyle was driving with enough pot and tequila in him to make even a familiar drive tenuous.

The bus and the Audi were on target to collide like they had before.

As the bus skidded onto the wet surface of the drawbridge, Kyle closed his eyes, ready to die for a greater purpose, but hoping to avoid his head exploding if he made eye contact with his younger self, who was driving the other car.

With the Audi only about thirty yards away, Kyle could feel the bus drifting.

"Hey!" Bruno's voice called out from behind him. "Watch where you're going."

Kyle no longer felt like he didn't deserve life, or happiness, but sacrificing himself was the only way he felt he could prove what he needed to to the Old Man. He hadn't made Kyle any promises, but Kyle hoped he was making a strong case for letting the human race continue.

The Audi was very close now. They were seconds from impact. *I'm ready*, Kyle said to himself.

"Hey!" a voice from behind him called out.

"Get back on our side of the road," another

one of the students yelled. Kyle felt a deep pang of guilt that he had to sacrifice the children too. But it was trying to undo his original mistake that had gotten him into this, and he could think of no way around the children dying too.

Moments before impact, Kyle had a horrible thought. He *had* failed to consider one crucial thing. He quickly pulled his seatbelt down over his lap and chest and clicked it in. He reached into his open backpack with one hand and pulled out his silk blot, holding the steering wheel with the other.

All of the bodies from the original crash had been recovered, Kyle remembered. He'd never thought about the fact that, if he was now going to be one of the people killed on the bus, the divers would discover his body too. It wouldn't take long to realize that there were two different versions of Kyle Cash involved with the crash—one dead on the bus, and one driving the Audi. *What if they find the silk blot?* Kyle thought to himself. *What if they somehow trace it back to the factory? What if finding me leads the world to find out about time weaving?*

He looked up as the Audi was only a few feet away. The kids let out screams and other sounds, partially in fear, and partially trying to implore Kyle to get onto his side of the road.

Kyle avoided looking at the driver's seat of the Audi. Even though he was about to die, he didn't want his head exploding. He could see Joe Stropoli, though, in the passenger seat as the Audi got within a few feet of the bus. He was pulling at 2014 Kyle's arm.

The kids on the bus saw the crash coming. There was a scream as soon as the driver's side of the bus slammed head-on into the driver's side of Joe's Audi, and then, as the bus lifted into the air, everything got silent.

As the bus turned like a log, rocketing over the guardrail on the drawbridge, time felt like it had stopped for him. Kyle felt great regret about not realizing his mistake sooner. If he died now, the secret of time weaving might not be safe. He braced against the steering wheel, hoping he could survive the impact now, whereas a few seconds ago, he wanted anything but that. The sound of the kids on the bus being thrown against the ceiling and then the side of bus ushered in more screams.

"Stay calm," Kyle yelled, even though it was hard to get the words out. When they hit the river below, water rushed in fast through Lisa's open window, and soon the bus was mostly filled with water. Kyle was surprised to see that most of the kids had survived the initial impact, just as he had. The bus bobbed for a short while, but Kyle could feel them beginning to sink.

There were screams, at first, but now when Kyle looked back, he saw the children trying to swim out through Lisa's window.

The bus sank below the water and Kyle held his breath. Once it began its descent, they fell quickly toward the bottom of the river. It didn't look like any of the children had made it out. Kyle looked back at the kids again. He knew the divers would recover their bodies so they could be buried properly. *How did I miss it?* he thought to himself as the pressure from the water began to press in on his ears. Kyle couldn't hold his breath any longer. He cursed himself once more for his stupidity. If he weren't underwater, he would've screamed as he pulled the silk blot over his head and entered the tunnel one more time.

CHAPTER 13

NOVEMBER 3, 2014

eight months after the crash, in kyle's original timestream

KYLE'S HEART RACED AS HE STEPPED DOWN OFF the prison bus, careful not to trip on the chain binding his feet together. The trick he'd learned for walking in shackles was to try not to think about them. When you did, taking the little shuffle steps you had to take became more difficult. Even looking at eight years behind bars, Kyle felt relieved to be finished with the entire legal process that followed the crash—his arrest, trial, and then the sentencing, which was the second-worst day of his life.

He'd needed to keep on a brave face for his mom, and even for Mr. Davidson, his lawyer, who never seemed to give up hope that Kyle could get off without serving any prison time. As soon as he'd recovered from his wounds and had been arraigned, though, Kyle had written off at least the next decade. He wouldn't even be eligible for parole for almost five years, but that was okay with him. It helped Kyle slightly with the intense guilt he felt over the deaths of the kids, their bus driver, and his best friend, Joe, that he would be forced to pay his debt. He'd had mixed emotions during the entire trial watching his lawyer try to blame everyone but Kyle for something that was obviously his fault—the brakes on the Audi, the rain, the city planning commission for a long delayed project that would've widened Banditt Drawbridge.

Even as he came to terms with it, the idea of losing the next eight years of his life was something Kyle needed to get used to all over again every day. Some mornings he woke up and could almost smell bacon cooking downstairs in his mother's house, only to be reminded of his surroundings when he opened his eyes. He'd never left New York State before, and had barely ever traveled beyond Flemming. All of the hard work Kyle put in during high school was irrelevant now. And when he got out of prison, his mistake would follow him forever.

Kyle stood in a line now with about twenty other new inmates, all of them in thin, orange jumpsuits, bouncing around to keep warm in the cold New York November. Once the gate leading to the prison's exterior had closed behind them, the driver left the prisoners standing there in the yard and walked inside Stevenson Youth Correctional, the building that would be Kyle's home for at least the beginning of his sentence. Kyle looked up and saw four guards with shotguns in the towers surrounding them. It would be a long time before Kyle did anything without someone watching him.

The prisoners were all around Kyle's age. He turned to get a look at the people behind him and caught a glimpse of one of the largest dudes he'd ever seen. He was a tall, Latin guy—maybe Puerto Rican, or Dominican. He looked like he could play in the NFL.

The second the door shut behind the driver, Kyle felt a shoulder hit him in his back. He turned around and saw a tough guy with a red goatee staring at him. The guy took a step closer to Kyle. "Why you lookin' at me, pussy faggot?"

Kyle ignored him and turned back around. Kyle wasn't sure how he was going to handle encounters like this while he did his time. He was a wiry stoner, not a fighter, and no one who looked at him would think otherwise.

"You turnin' your back on me now?" the kid with the red goatee asked, kicking Kyle in the back of the knee, nearly knocking him down.

"What the fuck?" Kyle said as he turned around, regretting it immediately.

Kyle heard two other white guys laughing, as the guy with the red goatee as he took a step toward him. "Oh shit, Braden's 'bout to fuck some shit up on his first day back," one of the guys said.

Braden raised his chained hands in the air together, turned, and backhanded Kyle's cheek, knocking him to the ground.

"Hey!" the mountainous Latin guy called out just as Braden was crouching over Kyle to take another shot.

Kyle skidded away on the ground and got back to his feet, just as two other Latin guys corralled the big guy, discouraging him from getting involved. "Ochoa, this ain't Latin business. Let the white boys handle their shit."

Kyle backed further and further away, hoping a guard would be out to bring them in soon. Then, he saw Ochoa push through his buddies and come up behind Braden. He grabbed Braden by the back of the neck, and Braden let out something that sounded like a yelp.

Ochoa brought his mouth toward Braden's ear from behind. "You want a problem? You got one right here." He kept squeezing and Kyle could see Braden's knees shaking.

"Oh, okay man," Braden said. "Just let go."

Ochoa slowly released the grip, and when Braden turned around, they stared at each other for a second. Kyle saw one of the two guys who knew Braden open his mouth and dig his fingers deep inside. He grabbed something small and rectangular, put it between two of his fingers and stepped toward Ochoa.

"Hey!" Kyle called out. "Behind you!"

Ochoa turned around just quickly enough to dodge out of the way as the guy swung at him with a razor blade.

Just then, the ground about ten feet to the side of everyone started crackling like Pop Rocks. Kyle turned and realized that one of the guards was shooting down toward them. A few seconds later, the shooting stopped. Then, a short and heavy older guard walked toward them. "Guys, knock it the fuck off," he said. "Little known fact about this place? We don't *have* to treat you fellas like animals. This is the time for a fresh start. But . . . if you force us to treat you like shit, then we will."

"Alright, pops," one of the guys called out, laughing.

The guard glared at him. "The name's Radbourn . . . Now you know it, so no excuse to be an asshole. Let's go."

The agitated group fell back into their line and followed Radbourn, threats flying back and forth, along with colorful descriptions of everyone's mothers.

Kyle had gotten lucky this time, but Ochoa, the Latin linebacker, probably wouldn't be there to save him next time.

"Yo, bro," Kyle heard someone behind him say. "Yo . . . white boy?"

Kyle still didn't turn around. He didn't want to get shot by a guard on this first day, or get into another fight.

"Yo . . . ? IRS . . . Beanpole . . . Vanilla Milkshake . . . Turn around."

Kyle finally looked halfway over his shoulder and saw Ochoa—the most relaxed guy in the line—trying to get his attention. Kyle looked at him, but tried not to keep eye contact for too long.

"Good lookin' out, bro," Ochoa said as they walked toward the door to the prison. "Good lookin' out."

CHAPTER 14

"THE TRUCK'S HERE," YOLANDA SAID TO SILLOW, as she walked into his office at the factory building. "Are we really gonna let the movers in here?"

Sillow nodded.

"Seems like it goes against everything we're supposed to do," Yolanda answered.

Sillow shrugged. If he'd told Yolanda what he was about to do, she would've tried to stop him. She didn't know anything about what Sillow had been doing late at night on the other floors of the factory building.

Kyle had come to see Sillow right before he went into the tunnel once more, leaving the factory for what was likely the final time, to tell him exactly what needed to happen. Sillow couldn't argue with the logic. If Kyle was trying to prove that the human race could stay out of the tunnel, then leaving the factory running and producing silk blots didn't make any sense.

Sillow had found meaning working in the factory that he'd never had before. As crazy and nonsensical as his life as a Sere was, it fit him much more than any of the jobs he'd had in the past. He'd been an orphan since his mother tragically died when he was two, and he suddenly had a family tradition. *Me, part of a "bloodline,"* Sillow thought to himself frequently. *How 'bout that?* Giving that up wouldn't be easy for him.

The next day was a Sunday. Everything that belonged to the family was in a huge truck bound for Florida. They'd rented a minivan for everyone except Sillow to make the trip. He told the family he'd join them in a few days, which he hoped was actually true.

He pulled out the stack of books he'd been hiding underneath one of the idle factory machines. He flipped to the index of *Applied Controlled Demolition* to check something. Kyle had given him a task he didn't think he could actually accomplish at first, but Sillow felt confident now that he was going to come through for his son again. It was just a matter of whether he could avoid getting arrested in the process.

Sillow took the elevator, slowly rumbling as it always did, down to the fourth floor and admired the haul he'd managed to procure in the past week. Because it was early Sunday morning in a part of New York City where most of the real estate was devoted to industrial space, Sillow hoped to go mostly undetected during this part of the operation.

He put on his orange vest and hardhat and

looked in a small mirror. *I'd buy it*, he thought to himself.

Then, he used a crowbar to get inside the buildings to the left and right of the factory building and went door-to-door. The building to the left of the factory was completely empty today, and after going through, he put cones in front of the entrance, and yellow caution tape over the door.

In the other neighboring building, Sillow encountered one older woman working in her fabric shop. At first, she wouldn't open the door for him, but when he told her there was a gas leak, she packed up quickly and left.

He put cones along the entire sidewalk, covering the length of all three buildings, and took the keys to two rented minivans out of his pocket. Once he lined them up to block the entire street, he'd have very little time before someone took notice of what was going on. Sunday morning or not, it *was* New York City, and cars passed in front of the factory building at regular intervals.

Sillow went upstairs to the fifth floor once more. Everything he'd owned before moving into the factory was on a truck heading to Florida, but he was about to destroy all traces of the time in his life he felt proudest about. Even Kyle was gone now.

There was the huge book that Sillow had begun translating which explained everything he knew about the Seres. He wanted desperately to take it with him, and tucked it under his arm. As long as he kept it hidden, there'd be no harm that could come from it, he thought. It was written in ancient Serican—no one would know what it was, and without the factory, there'd be no way to ever build a silk blot again.

He grabbed the remote charger, threw the book into a backpack, and headed downstairs. It made Sillow nervous to even hold the remote charger, so he did so very delicately, palming it in his hand with his fingers far from the buttons.

When he got outside, he eyed the sidewalk again with all of the cones and caution tape he'd lined up. The street was getting busier as it got later, and he needed to move quickly to avoid the chance of any bystanders getting killed.

Sillow got behind the wheel of one minivan parked in front of the factory and backed into the middle of the street. He parked perpendicular to the street, facing the building in front of him. Any car trying to pass in that direction would be blocked. He did the same with the other minivan in front of the other neighboring building. He'd effectively blocked off a perimeter around the factory building much larger than the blast radius he had calculated using the demolition textbooks he'd used for guidance.

Sillow got out of the second minivan and moved toward the street corner, looking back at the buildings to make sure no one crossed into his perimeter.

I can't believe I'm going to destroy this, he thought to himself. Even though he knew the reasoning was right—or, at least, Kyle believed it was—Sillow struggled with the idea of actually going through with it. The greatest secret humankind had ever known, and here he was making sure no one else would ever be able to use it.

Sillow stood safely away from the building on the street corner and gave one last check. He saw that no cars or pedestrians were close to the perimeter he'd set up. He had explosive packets, combinations of C4 and dynamite, on each floor of the building, with extra packets on each of the factory machines and inside the huge brick cylinder where they'd cultivated an environment of mulberry leaves with millions of silkworms. He took a deep breath and pressed the button on the remote charger he'd built himself from the instructions in one of the books.

He waited, cringing at the thought of the entire building coming down on top of itself. After a few seconds, he pressed the button again. Nothing.

Sillow remembered the book he'd used to build the charger. The equipment he'd used for the remote detonator was supposed to give him a range of one thousand feet, much longer than Sillow now stood from the building. He didn't even know how to detonate the explosives without the charger. Sillow regretted that he couldn't test the device earlier, but teaching himself as he went, he had no idea how he would've done that safely.

He walked toward the building, pressing the charger over and over as he got closer. Still nothing.

Now, he saw a taxi cab heading toward the perimeter. In a few seconds, it would be honking, unable to pass through Sillow's barrier. . .

Sillow ran toward the building, pressing the charger over and over, losing hope that it was only the range that he'd gotten wrong. It was completely possible that he'd built the charger wrong, or wired the explosives incorrectly. Of all the times he wanted to come through for his son, he wanted now to make sure Kyle's sacrifice was for a purpose.

He pushed the button again and again. Hopelessness crept in as he moved very close to one of the minivans. Suddenly, he heard something click. Then, he saw the top floor of the factory building explode outward, debris raining toward the street below. Sillow turned and started running away from the building as fast as he could.

A few seconds later, he felt a blast of heat at his back, the force throwing him to the street. Sillow looked back at the building and saw exactly what he'd hoped. The entire front of the factory building was gone, and the insides looked completely destroyed. There were some small active fires inside, but it wasn't an inferno, which had been Sillow's goal. Before he even got up off the ground and ran, hoping to get to the car he'd parked on the next block, he heard sirens coming toward the building.

Sillow ran down the street, but noticed that something felt different. Lighter. He took off his backpack and saw that the bag had been destroyed. The book of Seres's secrets he'd taken was gone. He turned back. Even though he'd convinced himself he wasn't doing anything terrible by preserving the book, he didn't want it winding up in someone else's hands. Then, he saw it right next to one of the minivans, burning in the middle of the street. To activate the charger, Sillow had needed to come just close enough to the explosion for it to singe the backpack he was wearing. And now, like the factory building, the book of Sere secrets would only exist in the past.

Ain't that something? Sillow thought to himself as he ran down the street toward his car.

CHAPTER 15

FEBRUARY 22, 2022

four years later

ALLAIRE GOT OUT OF THE PASSENGER SEAT OF her squad car and drew her Glock 19. Her new partner, Jason Bennett, popped out of the driver's seat, his gun drawn too.

The call over their radio said that a pedestrian heard shots fired inside the abandoned Loew's Multiplex in downtown Jacksonville. Shuttered since before Allaire ever left New York, the department got a call about something going on inside the empty theater every few weeks.

They knew the easiest entrance to the building was a side door leading directly to one of the movie theaters, accessible from the alley next to the building.

Dear Kyle,

Life is different now.

I've found a way to make myself useful to the people around me. It'll never measure up to you saving the universe, and the little part of that I maybe helped with, but when the world didn't end after you left, I had to do something with the rest of my life, right . . . ?

Allaire entered the largest theater with her partner right behind her. She'd been in so many of these situations with Ayers—drawn into a dark and dangerous space—that she wondered sometimes whether she had *enough* fear to make sure she didn't get herself killed.

Bennett pointed up at the projector room. They'd found junkies in there before. Usually, though, the junkies weren't carrying weapons. The call on their radio had made it sound like some kind of gunfight had happened.

Again, Allaire led the way as the two cops headed up the steps to the projector room. Allaire shined her flashlight on the stairs when she noticed they felt slick. She pointed her light down and saw blood below her feet. She pushed the door open and held her gun in front of her. She turned the flashlight into the room and saw a man laying on the ground, unconscious, with several bullet wounds. The blood on the stairs told her that he was shot somewhere else and had escaped to the projector room.

Some days, though, it feels like I'm on a hamster wheel. The people who don't follow the rules aren't ever going to follow them. I'm just here to make sure it doesn't get out of hand . . . In some ways, it's not all that different from our old life. Our life. It hurts to think about having a life with you. I know it shouldn't, and I should be happy for the time we had. But, it does . . .

"Radio in for backup," Allaire said to Bennett. "Stay with this guy."

"You got it, Officer Cash," Bennett answered.

Allaire raced out of the projector room, and down the stairs to look for the shooter. She went up and down the aisles of the theater looking, but didn't see anything. Then, she left the theater and found herself in the lobby.

She checked most of the usual spots where they'd found junkies before when they'd cleared the theater—behind the concession area, and inside the smaller theaters—but there was no one.

Now, she kicked open the door to the women's restroom, and didn't see anyone in there either. "Not sure our shooter's still in here," she said to Bennett over the radio.

She walked toward the men's bathroom now to

check inside, but stopped. Bennett hadn't answered her. "Hey, Jay, you there?"

When he didn't answer again, Allaire ran back toward the large theater and raced up the stairs toward the projector room.

Working with a partner has taken some getting used to. Well, working with a partner who isn't you. I've had to learn to trust a lot more than I ever have before, not only at work . . .

When Allaire pushed into the projector room, a tall kid with a white t-shirt was pointing a gun at her partner. He moved the gun toward Allaire for a second and then back toward Bennett.

"Toss your gun over there," the kid said. Allaire could see that Bennett's gun was already on the floor.

"Hey, kid," Allaire said. "No problem. You got it. You're in charge." She slowly laid her gun down on the floor as the kid trained his gun on Bennett.

"This ain't none of your business," the kid said. "That muthafucka owed me money. A lot."

"Why don't you let us go?" Allaire asked. "We'll leave, and you can get a head start on the cops."

"You're the cops!" the kid said. Allaire could see that his hands were shaky. She'd learned enough in her time on the force to know that you didn't want to trust a tweaker to be rational. She needed to get the two of them out of there.

Allaire nodded. "How about this? You let my partner go, and keep me as your hostage for now. No one's gonna come at you in here if you have a cop as a hostage . . ."

The kid looked like he was thinking about it. He kept moving the gun from Allaire to Bennett and then back.

Allaire could almost time his movements back and forth. *One . . . Two . . . Three . . . Four . . . Point at me . . . One . . . Two . . . Three . . . Four . . . Point at Bennett.*

The guy already seemed to have forgotten what

Allaire proposed. He started breathing deeper. Allaire was afraid he was going to do something stupid.

At first, they didn't want me to carry my karambit blade. I needed special permission, and it was only for the purpose of cutting clothing, seatbelts, or other inanimate objects. Police aren't trained with knives, so it's against the rules to use them as a weapon in the field. I never had any intention of breaking the rule . . .

One . . . Two . . . Three . . . Four . . . As soon as the kid turned with the gun toward Bennett, Allaire moved stealthily behind him, and brought her karambit up to the soft spot on his neck. She'd produced it instantly from her side pocket where she'd kept it every day since her first as a cop.

"Drop the gun," she said to the kid.

At first the kid just froze.

Bennett's face was a mix of fear and surprise.

Allaire pressed the knife harder against the kid's neck. "Please, drop it, kid."

The kid got jittery and began shaking the gun. Bennett stepped around him, away from the barrel, and was able to get the gun out of the kid's hands.

Allaire quickly closed the karambit blade and slid it back into her pants pocket. She pulled her handcuffs from her belt and slapped them on the kid's wrists.

When it's life or death, you have to use every tool at your disposal, even if it's not listed in a rulebook. You and I never knew the rules. We just had to guess and hope we were right.

I hope I'm right about you, Kyle. I hope that, in some distant timestream out there, you'll be eligible for parole soon. That you can have a normal life. Meet someone (your own age!) and have a family. I know you're smart enough not to let the bus crash ruin the rest of your life. When Sillow first destroyed the factory, I hated him for it. I couldn't believe that you

were really gone from our timestream. But, I know
now that all the silk blots in the world wouldn't be
able to get me to you. If there were some way to find
you, I don't think I could resist. And, eventually, I
think the kids would come looking for you too.

Later that night, Allaire got out of the shower
and walked downstairs to the living room. Sillow's
daughters, Tinsley and Larkin, each sat in a love-
seat doing homework. Demetrius climbed on top
of Sillow, wrestling with his grandpa. The four-
year-old looked like a miniature version of Kyle,
but with Allaire's light hair.

When Demetrius saw his mom, he jumped off
of Sillow and ran up to her. "Can you do our stories tonight?"

Allaire smiled at her older son, happy to be
home for bedtime. She was still wound up from
work, though, and the calmness of home was
almost overwhelming to her in that moment. "Of
course . . . Where's your brother?"

"Yolanda's giving him a snack," Sillow said. "If the kid would eat some real food, he wouldn't need an after-dinner snack."

Allaire shrugged, and walked into the kitchen.

Some days, it's really hard adjusting to regular life. There's a lot to love about it. But, it doesn't feel real to me. I keep waiting for something to happen. For some other shoe to drop. But, it hasn't. Accepting that everything is going to be okay is hard sometimes. Maybe that's crazy, but you're the person who knows my craziness best.

Allaire walked into the kitchen and kissed Browning on the head. Her younger son was a moose, almost as big as his brother already, which only made people more likely to mistake them for twins.

"Hi, Mama," he said.

"Grandpa said you didn't eat dinner again," Allaire said.

Browning scrunched his face up. "I hate lasagna."

"Hate's a strong word, sweetie," Allaire said.

"It had spinach," Browning answered.

I wish you could've met Browning. He's more like you than anyone I've ever met. He has the same devil-may-care look in his eye, until he thinks he's upset you. And then he can't bear it. He's my tough teddy bear. And, your last gift to me.

Later that evening, Allaire sat on the floor beneath the boys' bunk beds. They were snuggled on each side of her, tired from the day, but fighting it.

"One more story," Demetrius said.

"One from your head," Browning answered.

Demetrius bounced excitedly. "Yeah!"

"Okay," Allaire answered.

"About Dad," Demetrius said, "and the mean Old Man."

The boys know everything. They just have no idea it's all real. It's a strange thing to see all of our history turned into fiction. They think I'm the best storyteller ever. Sometimes I wonder if it actually was real. Silk blots, time tunnels, crazy ancient traditions . . . All of it. But then I look at their faces, and I think of yours, and I know that you'd be here if it weren't real. If you'd had any choice at all.

Once Demetrius and Browning were both asleep, Allaire crept out of their room and into hers. She lit a couple of candles and changed into her pajamas.

Allaire picked up a pad and pen from her night table, and continued her letter to Kyle.

I admit it. I still have hope. I know I shouldn't, but I do.

Sometimes, I'll hear a noise in the house, and I'm convinced it's you. Or, when I'm driving my patrol car, I'll see someone sitting at a bus stop, or pass in a car, and I'll wonder if you've come just to get a glimpse of me and your sons.

I hope you're okay, Kyle. Somewhere, somehow, maybe you—the Kyle I knew—found a way to survive. I'm not dumb enough to think anything's impossible anymore. I prefer believing, Kyle. Believing in you.

I miss and love you. Endlessly.

Love Always,

Allaire

Allaire stood up when she finished her note and walked over to the candles near her mirror. She looked in the mirror and wondered whether Kyle would still think she was beautiful. She looked harder than she had before he left. The years were really starting to show on her face. Raising both boys without Kyle, and having to rebuild her life in the real world, hadn't always been easy. She looked at herself again, as she held the letter up to the candle.

Of course he'd think I was beautiful, she thought to herself and smiled. She'd been able to count on so few things in her life, but she could always count on Kyle.

The letter burned in her hand at first, and when the heat got to be too much, she walked over to the metal garbage can in the corner of her room and tossed it in. She watched the last of the paper get swallowed by the flames before she turned away and went to bed.

CHAPTER 16

OUTSIDE OF TIME

As before, it only took Kyle a few minutes to pound through the tunnel with his paddle. He climbed out and knew immediately that all eyes were on him.

Last time, he'd come out to a construction zone—thousands of people busy with dismantling the tunnel with tools and machines. This time, it felt different. There were still just as many people on the beach near the tunnel, but they were idle. They stood around, or sat in the sand. Kyle had hoped to see them reconstructing the tunnel. It was why he'd left his family, and chosen to go back to the day of the original bus crash.

Kyle spotted the hill where he'd spoken to the Old Man, and started walking in that direction. But, before he could get off the beach, though, Simyon was there, blocking his way.

"You weren't supposed to come back," Simyon said. "We've been waiting for him to tell us what to do next. This isn't going to help . . . "

Kyle tried pushing past Simyon. "I need to see him."

Simyon put his hand on Kyle's chest.

"Let me go," Kyle said.

"He doesn't want to see you," Simyon said.

Kyle pushed Simyon hard, sending him backward into the sand.

"No, no, no," Simyon called out after him. "You don't get to do this."

Kyle walked toward the grassy hill, but didn't see the Old Man.

Simyon chased after Kyle and grabbed his arm. "He's not just someone you can visit whenever you want. You're breaking every rule we have here."

"There are no rules," Kyle said. "It's all a set up. Don't you get it? This whole thing. He's just trying to keep people from the other side from getting here. That's all. The rules. The reasons. It's all for that. That's it."

Simyon stood between Kyle and the hill again and nodded emphatically. "Exactly! And you're here! Don't you see the problem? He's going to get rid of the tunnel, and we're not going to have any work left . . . And then all of *my* people become expendable. I've seen what he does when he doesn't want something around anymore."

Kyle pushed past Simyon again, and Simyon grabbed his arm. Kyle felt a sudden burst of heat coming through Simyon's hand and tried to pull his arm away. Kyle turned to him and saw Simyon's head beginning to expand, like Ochoa's and Young Ayers's had right before they exploded. Simyon quickly removed his hand from Kyle and turned away from him. He looked back at Kyle and swatted the air as he walked away.

When Kyle turned around, the Old Man was standing on the hill.

"You're back," the Old Man said, sitting down in the grass. "I didn't expect that."

"I'm not dead, am I?" Kyle asked, sitting down next to the Old Man in the grass.

"Are you?" the Old Man answered.

"I felt myself starting to drown," Kyle said. "But then I realized my mistake—"

"And what was that?" the Old Man said.

"I thought that just being on the bus, and making the crash happen like it did before, would make everything okay."

"You're very concerned with that," the Old Man said.

"With what?" Kyle asked.

"With making everything okay," the Old Man answered. "You always have been."

"But then, I realized that they'd find my body under the water," Kyle said. "And then, who knows?

People would wonder why there were two versions of me involved with the crash."

"They would," the Old Man said.

"And wouldn't that be a problem?" Kyle asked.

The Old Man shook his head. "I've told you that what you do on the other side is of very little consequence to me. I just want people to stay out of the tunnel."

"But, I thought people might get suspicious. Maybe they'd find the factory. Or find this place," Kyle said, hoping for a look of understanding from the Old Man.

"Seems like these are very remote possibilities," the Old Man answered.

Kyle wondered why the Old Man wasn't understanding. "I'm just hoping you can see my sacrifice, and then maybe, you'll start rebuilding the tunnel."

"We *were* rebuilding," the Old Man said.

"*Were?*" Kyle asked.

"And, then you came here," the Old Man said. "You weren't supposed to do that."

"I don't understand," Kyle said.

The Old Man smiled. "You would've gone into the tunnel *again,* too, if you hadn't thrown water on your son's face . . . There's so much that you don't understand, Kyle. Too much, I'm afraid."

"Tell me, then," Kyle said.

The Old Man was silent for once. He looked out at the people on the beach. Thousands of them with their eyes fixed on their conversation.

"Is everything okay?" Kyle continued. "On the other side?"

"There's that word again," the Old Man said. "Okay."

The Old Man lay back on his elbows in the grass. He was either oblivious, or he almost enjoyed their audience of thousands, each of them desperate for his direction.

"Just relax for a minute," the Old Man said.

"I don't understand," Kyle said. "I need you to tell me what I'm supposed to do."

The Old Man looked at Kyle, examining his

face. He looked down the hill at Simyon's people. Kyle couldn't begin to guess what he was thinking.

"Come on then," the Old Man said, slowly standing up.

The Old Man led Kyle to the trees above the hillside. "I need to keep this shrubbery thick. People need to believe there's some mystical reason they can't cross it."

"Who *are* you?" Kyle asked.

The Old Man smirked as he led Kyle through the forest of trees. Although there was complete tree cover, somehow the purple light of the sky shined through, giving the leaves a tint that was unlike anything Kyle had ever seen. It felt like they'd walked for hours by the time the trees thinned out.

The Old Man turned to him and cocked his head. "I've never brought anyone here."

"I need to know if I fixed everything," Kyle said, not wanting to step through the last of the trees. He didn't want to have any knowledge that would stop the Old Man from letting him go back to Earth.

"No, you haven't fixed anything," the Old Man answered. He walked up to Kyle and they sat on the same stump. "Do you remember where you started?"

Kyle nodded. "I don't need to see what you're going to show me. I just want to make everything okay for Allaire and our son."

"Sons," the Old Man said.

"Really?" Kyle asked.

"That last time you were with her," the Old Man said.

Kyle's heart sank. He'd only met Demetrius as a newborn, and now, he learned that he had another son.

"Is there any way I can go back?" Kyle asked, tears filling his eyes. "I grew up without a father. I know what it's like."

The Old Man put his hand on Kyle's shoulder and squeezed, a little too hard. He leaned his mouth to Kyle's ear. "Don't you remember the promise you made me?"

Kyle nodded.

"Would you really destroy humanity if I go back?" Kyle asked.

The Old Man nodded and stood up. "I've done it before . . . Come with me."

Kyle followed the Old Man through the last of the trees and they reached the bottom of a very steep hill. This one was made of dirt.

"Careful climbing," the Old Man said, before expertly scaling the hill.

Like the trees, the hill felt endless to Kyle. The Old Man looked unaffected from the climb, while Kyle was dripping with sweat.

The Old Man sat at the top of the hill with his knees pulled to his chest.

Kyle looked out and saw an endless expanse in front of him, with huge trenches of various lengths carved into the ground. Some of the trenches were filled with deep, black metal tunnels. Others were empty. Some of the tunnels were covered with green vines and brown branches. Some of the trenches looked like they'd been scorched, with smoke rising into the air.

It took Kyle a few minutes to take in the enormity of it all, stretching beyond where he could see in every direction. He pondered all of humanity in that moment. The way people live and understand the universe—it was all based on assumptions that just weren't true. This behind-the-scenes view was so oddly different than anyone could have ever imagined. And Kyle, of all people, was being let in on this great secret.

The Old Man turned backward and pointed at one of the trenches, half filled with a tunnel. "That's your world," he said. "They'd rebuilt to about 2050 before I saw you get into that silk blot again."

"But, I explained why I did it," Kyle said. "They would've found me under the water."

"So what?" the Old Man said. "There are a lot

of mysteries in your world. Your death would have just been another. You've missed the whole point, Kyle."

"I'm . . . I'm sorry," Kyle said.

The Old Man shook his head. "It just proved my point. Your people always think they know best, and you couldn't resist trying to fix a problem by using the tunnel . . . For all of his weakness, Simyon the rebel can listen . . . You, sons of Umar, not so much."

"I don't know what to say," Kyle said.

"Everyone is looking for meaning," the Old Man said, "when most of the time, the simplest answer is the right one. If people would just follow the rules, instead of questioning them, they'd be a lot better off . . . Do you know why I told your people that second sons were cursed?"

Kyle shook his head. Of course, he didn't know.

"Because ensuring that there were only enough Seres to carry on the bloodline meant fewer people would enter the tunnel," the Old Man said.

"The simplest answer," Kyle said.

"Now you've got it," the Old Man said.

Kyle looked out onto the vast network of trenches and tunnels. "Is this the entire universe?"

"What do you think?" the Old Man asked.

Kyle shook his head. "No . . . You can't just show me this, and then ask me to figure it out for myself."

"You've been figuring it out for yourself ever since you first went inside a silk blot," the Old Man said.

"Why do they all look different?" Kyle asked. "Some have tunnels. Some don't."

"Some of them are just beginning," the Old Man said. "Some are finished. Most are somewhere in the middle."

"Are these different timestreams?" Kyle asked.

"They're every possible outcome of every choice made by every single being ever to live."

Kyle looked in the distance. The extent of the

trenches seemed endless. "How big is all of this? How long does it go on?"

"It doesn't end," the Old Man said. "What you can see here is the equivalent of a grain of sand on the beach."

"Who created this?" Kyle asked. "Who built all of this?"

"Who do you think?" the Old Man asked.

Then, the Old Man brought his hand into the air and pointed at an empty trench in the distance. Suddenly, right before Kyle's eyes, a huge tunnel appeared piece by piece, covered by branches and leaves. The purple sky above them flashed and Kyle watched the tunnel shimmer for a moment in the same liquidy way that a silk blot did. "Finally, life on Saturn."

"Just like that?" Kyle asked, amazed that the Old Man had created a tunnel with a wave of his hand.

The Old Man shrugged. "You can't sit and ponder it all too much . . . Sometimes you just have to take action."

"So, if you just built that yourself," Kyle said, "what about the people on the beach? Why are they building the tunnel?"

"Your world is unique," the Old Man said. "No one's ever broken through from any of these other worlds. Before Simyon and his brother, I didn't even use tunnels. I thought the trenches were enough."

Kyle looked down at his timestream, the only part of the vast landscape in front of him with any sign of life. "But why keep those people there? If you can just build the tunnel yourself, then—"

"I needed to learn about your people," the Old Man said. "You'd developed past where you were supposed to. That's never happened before . . . And *they* needed to learn. I sent Simyon's brother back to make sure no one else broke through, but everything he did led to you eventually getting here anyway. Interesting isn't it?"

Kyle sat on the hill and shook his head. The entire thing was beyond comprehension to him.

"What's that one?" Kyle asked, pointing at a very short tunnel in the distance.

"That's a young planet in a galaxy billions of light years from yours," the Old Man said.

"And that one?" Kyle asked, pointing at another. This one was a long trench, with no tunnel.

"That one is part of your world," the Old Man said. "Or, at least, it will be. Millions of years from now. Three cataclysms away."

"Cataclysms?" Kyle asked.

"Resets," the Old Man answered. "Like the dinosaurs, or the Ice Age . . . It's your world, but it's a different part. A different era."

"Can I stop it?" Kyle asked.

The Old Man laughed. "Very ambitious of you to ask," the Old Man said. "Resets are nothing to trouble yourself with. Every one of these trenches ends somewhere . . . Some of their worlds come back many years later, and others become cosmic dust. A tree has many leaves, and one of them may fall to the ground. Another one grows. Another one falls. A tree dies, a tree is born. And on and on and on . . . "

Kyle sat for a long time next to the Old Man taking in the whole of everything that had existed, and everything that would ever exist. He looked upon the timelines of some places mankind dreamed of going, and other places humans didn't even know to conceive of. There were billions of people on Earth alone, and Kyle wondered how many trillions—or more—made up all of the living creatures accounted for by the trenches and tunnels in front of him.

But after a while, even with the entire universe in front of him, Kyle turned back to the tunnel which led to the world he knew. It was the path back to Allaire and his two sons. It was the path back to the bus crash as well. It was time to return to his world.

CHAPTER 17

INSIDE THE TUNNEL

KYLE KNELT IN THE TUNNEL AND TRACED THE rung labeled *2017* with his finger. This was the year where he'd left Allaire, Demetrius and their unborn son, along with Sillow and his family. If Kyle exited the tunnel here, he knew he'd spend whatever time they had left happy. Perhaps the Old Man was bluffing, Kyle thought, but probably not. Perhaps Kyle could go back to his life here, just stop making silk blots, and the Old Man would decide to keep his world spinning along.

But, Kyle thought about the charred trenches among the infinite worlds and timestreams the Old Man showed him. Kyle worried that he could be signing a death warrant for every future family to exist on Earth if he went back to spend whatever time he could with his. If the simplest answer was the right one, then the Old Man was indeed planning to do what he said he would and dismantle the tunnel unless Kyle did what he promised.

He was tempted to go back for just a few minutes. Just to look in on them . . . But he knew if he exited the silk blot here, he'd never come back again.

Instead, Kyle continued to trace with his finger across the rung and thought of everything he'd seen and done since first entering a silk blot: *getting to know Sillow, stopping the bus crash, falling in love with Allaire, resisting and defeating Ayers, meeting Demetrius, and encountering the mysterious Old Man who showed him the secrets of the entire universe.*

Kyle cried for a few minutes. It was a cry of finality. He hoped Allaire could make the boys believe he hadn't left them by choice. Because he *didn't* have a choice. He knew that now.

CHAPTER 18

MARCH 13, 2014

the morning of the bus crash

KYLE TUNED OUT THE NOISE OF THE CHILDREN sitting behind him as he drove the bus down the hill toward Banditt Drawbridge.

This time he touched the brake only enough to make sure he didn't run off the road before he saw Joe's Audi coming in the other direction. He hadn't had the time to get used to wearing the leg and arm weights, so calibrating something like his pressure on the brake while coming down Nairn Boulevard was more difficult than normal.

They reached the bottom of the hill and Kyle watched the high school zoom by on his left. He'd never set foot inside again after the original bus crash, but he knew it would be safe now. After all of his time weaving, the original outcome was the right one. And, Kyle knew now, it was the only one that there could be. Even with the heavy weights attached to his upper arms like water wings, concealed by his baggy sweatshirt, his body shook with nervousness. He wished his hands were crazy-glued to the steering wheel.

Kyle spotted the Audi far in the distance now, racing down the other hill across the bridge. He reflexively grabbed for his seatbelt, but stopped himself, and instead cranked his window down.

Kyle replayed the dumb conversation he and Joe had on that morning—the last words Joe ever spoke. *What if I hadn't been distracted by Joe's self-pity, and never took my eyes off the road?* Kyle wondered to himself. *What if the bus crash never happened?*

Kyle couldn't help but recognize the irony in his question. After all, he *knew* a world in which the crash never happened. But Kyle knew now that just because you changed the past, you couldn't erase it. The threads of everything that had happened in every timestream still lingered, and impacted new timestreams in ways Kyle would never fully understand.

A few seconds later, the Audi was in full view and quickly moving toward the bus, having picked up speed coming down the hill. Kyle picked up a pair of binoculars from his open backpack next to him. The weights on his arms made it harder to hold the binoculars up to his eyes as he drove, causing him to swerve the bus over the yellow line a couple of times.

Kyle spotted the 2014 version of himself still looking ahead as he drove, and his heart started to race. *There I am!* Kyle thought to himself. The boy in the Audi was obviously younger, but also unburdened, for a few more seconds. Kyle's head began to hurt as he looked at his younger self through the binoculars. He struggled to keep a grip on the steering wheel as the pain became more intense.

He knew from experiencing the crash *as* the 2014 Kyle, that his younger self never had a chance to look at the driver of the bus. Kyle just needed to make sure he could keep his eyes on 2014 Kyle for long enough. He could feel his head swelling as the Audi got within a few car lengths of the bus.

The pressure in his head quickly became unbearable and Kyle let out a scream. If the next few seconds went according to what he had planned, he would float to the bottom of Banditt River, his body likely never to be discovered by the divers who pulled up the children who died in the crash. And, if his body was discovered, Kyle's hope was that without teeth or fingerprints, his identity would never be discovered. The Old Man hadn't seemed concerned, but Kyle knew this was the safest way.

Kyle gritted his teeth from the agonizing pain. It was almost over now, and he knew it was safe to drop the binoculars. The last thing Kyle managed to do was give the wheel of the bus a huge turn to the left, slamming right into the Audi. He then brought his hands up to his head just as it blew off of his body. In his last conscious moment, just as the bus flew into the air, he felt his hands, which had been covering his head, tear off from the explosive force as well.

CHAPTER 19

AUGUST 19, 2065

fifty-one years later

DEMETRIUS PULLED HIS CAR TO A STOP ALONG A steep hill.

"Pull into the parking lot, dummy," Browning said.

Demetrius gave his brother a look. He didn't take anything seriously. Demetrius pulled the key from the ignition and popped out of the car, pressing the sun protection button on his glasses. As the world darkened exactly to his liking, Demetrius walked toward the school.

Browning exited the passenger side of the car, holding the unassuming silver urn their mother had picked out for her ashes long before she'd actually died.

"Amazing that a whole person can fit in there, isn't it . . . ? Remind me why we're here again?" Browning asked his brother as they walked toward the grassy field.

"This is the one, right?" Demetrius asked.

"Well, there's the high school," Browning said, pointing to the ancient looking school building. "So this must be the field . . . You think they *did it* here?"

Demetrius shrugged. "Dude, I don't know . . . She said it wasn't where she met Dad, but that it was an important place to the two of them . . . Have just a little respect, would you?"

"It's just a weird choice is all," Browning answered.

Demetrius shook his head. His brother had come along kicking and screaming, but Demetrius knew his brother's humor was just masking how hard this was for him.

"So . . . anywhere here?" Browning asked.

"Let's walk until it feels right," Demetrius said. He'd asked his brother before if he got the same kinds of feelings he did and Browning either didn't, or wouldn't admit it. But Demetrius just *felt* things sometimes. Especially when it came to their father. There were just times Demetrius could almost sense that he was there with him. He thought these strange feelings probably accounted for the fact that he had always taken a more charitable outlook on their dad's absence than Browning had. Demetrius truly had faith that his mother was telling the truth when she told them their father was heroic. Browning would usually scoff at the idea that their father had been forced to sacrifice his life to save the rest of the world.

They walked for a while, Demetrius trying to will himself to feel something he just wasn't. "I don't feel anything yet."

"You know they were all just bedtime stories," Browning said. "Don't you? The idea that Dad might be alive in some other dimension, and that's why we can feel him sometimes. It's all bullshit that helped her accept him leaving."

Demetrius ignored his brother and walked a little further. He did feel things sometimes. He didn't know why, and he couldn't really explain them to someone who didn't feel them. The wind picked up a bit and a plastic take out container blew in front of the brothers as they walked.

"The tunnel, and that bad guy, Ayers," Browning said. "Mom was creative. A little crazy, too, if you ask me."

A few seconds later, Demetrius came to a spot far from the school's parking lot, and far from the school itself. He didn't know why he felt like they needed to stop, but he did. "This is it. This is where we do it."

Browning nodded. Demetrius could see that his brother was trying hard to keep it together and didn't blame him for running his mouth. That was how he coped with sadness.

"What now?" Browning asked, his mood suddenly more somber.

Demetrius took the urn from his brother, but immediately regretted it. As soon as they spread her ashes, she'd really be gone. The last physical piece of her, at least, would no longer be in their possession.

Browning took the folded envelope out of his pocket. They'd promised their mother that they wouldn't open it until they got here. He pulled the tab open and pulled out two pieces of paper. As Browning silently read the first, Demetrius saw his brother break down. Browning brought one hand to his face, and then fell to his knees, the paper still in his hand. Demetrius sat next to him on the ground and put his hand on his back as his brother cried. The wind was blowing the paper in Browning's hand in just such a way that Demetrius couldn't see what it said.

"I'm okay," Browning said, standing up and beginning to compose himself. "Here, you read it."

Demetrius took the two papers from his brother, and the second he read their mother's words, his eyes filled with tears as well. He thought about how children couldn't really ever understand what their parents felt until so many years later. Until they had kids of their own, like Demetrius did now.

"Okay," Demetrius said, clearing his throat. "Here lies Allaire Cash, who finally belonged. To Kyle. To Demetrius. To Browning."

Demetrius poured out half of the ashes before handing the urn to his brother.

As Browning poured out the remainder of their mother's ashes, which quickly scattered in the wind, Demetrius felt his father's presence more than ever before. He imagined him there, with their mother, falling in love as they planned to save the world. Or, maybe not even planning to, but saving it anyway. He had no way of knowing which of his mother's crazy stories were real, but today, he was open to believing any of them.

Once the ashes were spread, Demetrius put the

top back on the urn and flipped to the second piece of paper. There were a series of numbers: 02-03-98.

"What's it say?" Browning asked, his petulant mood gone now, after a cathartic cry.

Demetrius showed him the paper.

"February 3rd, 1998?" Browning asked.

"Did you ever figure out the combination to the safe in her apartment?" Demetrius asked.

"She said she left the combination somewhere, but never said where," Browning answered. "I forgot all about it."

Demetrius was too curious to go home, and without even discussing it with his brother, he drove them straight to their mother's apartment in Manhattan after they spread her ashes in Flemming.

They quickly found street parking and headed upstairs. The apartment had always felt spare.

She'd never owned a television, only had a few books—all non-fiction, and added very few decorative elements over the years. The boys joked sometimes about how their mother's knife collection was her most prized possession. To the day she died, she wore a knife clipped to her side. She always said it was just an old habit and felt weird not to have. But, the way her hand would unconsciously hover right over the blade after she was startled awake, or heard a loud noise, told the story of someone who feared her past might eventually catch up with her.

Browning pushed in front of Demetrius and headed into her bedroom closet. He slid her clothing to the side and they looked at the door of the safe. "What if there's money in here?"

"That'd be nice," Demetrius answered, but he doubted it. Their mother had given them everything she had before she passed. She'd been lucky enough—if you could call it that—to know a few months before that the cancer would eventually end her life, so she'd been able to get all of her limited affairs in order.

Browning keyed in the numbers and the safe clicked unlocked. He pulled it open and there was only one item inside. Browning pulled it out and stepped backward toward his brother, holding the thing in front of both of them.

It was a thin piece of rounded fabric with a deep sheen to it. So deep, it seemed almost like the brightness was coming from inside. As Browning held it in his hands, it shuddered, rippling just a little like when you throw a pebble into a pond.

"You know what this is?" Demetrius asked, looking his brother in the eye.

"Holy fuck," Browning said, in total shock. "Of course I know what it is. I listened to her stories too . . . I just never believed them."

Demetrius knew he shouldn't, but he couldn't resist. He poked his finger, then his hand, through the material, and smiled, wondering how many times their mother and father had done exactly the same thing.

THE END